HEAVENLY TALES

To: Dear Kathleen

With my sincere thanks for a wonderful friendship over many years and so much help with my family history.

With love — Martin

Published under licence by Brown Dog Books and
The Self-Publishing Partnership, 7 Green Park Station, Bath BA1 1JB

www.selfpublishingpartnership.co.uk

ISBN printed book: 978-1-83952-267-3
ISBN e-book: 978-1-83952-268-0

Cover design by Kevin Rylands
Internal design by Andrew Easton

Printed and bound in the UK

This book is printed on FSC certified paper

HEAVENLY TALES

M. B. EVANS

HEAVENLY TALES

The following stories are about mankind and an imaginary heaven in which angels and saints feature predominantly. It should be noted that this heaven and the characters described here do not exactly relate to the conventional Christian heaven, but since mankind was made in the image of God some resemblance is inevitable, or so it is believed.

M. B. Evans

TABLE OF CONTENTS

1

IN THE BEGINNING

It is not generally realised that God is a committee. Hitherto it has always been assumed that God is a single being: a being both omnipotent and benevolent, a being who is looking after every single individual on the earth and all the other species that exist on the billions of other planets in the billions of other star systems. It is rather a large job for a single entity. Common sense dictates, therefore, that God must have help and indeed God does have help. He is a committee, or at least he is the senior entity controlling a committee. He delegates but his is the ultimate authority. He is so senior, in fact, and his opinions carry so much weight that to all intents and purposes he is a committee.

In the beginning God had a difficult time with his creation, which he had called the earth. He had been very careful with this world and spent much time on details. The islands of the world and the Greek islands in particular had given him much trouble. On mature reflection, however, he thought there were too many islands, each with its own endless creeks and inlets, and it would have been far better to have designed a few large land masses rather than so many small ones. Volcanoes were a problem too. They would keep bursting forth and spoiling the landscapes he had already designed and created. The movement of the earth's tectonic plates also caused huge changes in the land masses and one particular clash of these plates had resulted in Mount Snowdon (as it was eventually called) being one hundred thousand feet high, far higher than God had intended. He felt rightly that one gigantic mountain spoiled the symmetry of the world. Then, since he couldn't be bothered to wipe it all out and start again, he introduced weathering in the form of a sizeable amount of water. The action of water through its weathering processes reduced ridiculously high lumps of land to more manageable proportions. It was a good idea and solved a lot of problems. Another difficulty it resolved was associated with the huge numbers of animals and plants he had created to decorate his new world. They required a regular intake of working fluids to ensure their well-being and water was the ideal material for that as well. Once created, however, all these life forms needed constant monitoring and to save himself time and energy he invented evolution. History has erroneously recorded that evolution was first described by Charles Darwin but the whole concept was God's and his alone. It was rather irksome for God to be constantly reminded that the credit for his work was attributed to a mere human being.

During the millions of years since the world had been

formed, it had undergone many changes and was almost unrecognisable from the originally created world. These changes were the result of God's changes of mind and his love of tinkering with his creation. The world had become a sort of experimental planet where God could observe the effect of any major or minor changes he fancied. The extinction of the dinosaurs was an example of this when he had decided to try out a new form of thunderbolt and found it to be more effective than he had originally planned. The ice ages, too, were an experiment in climate control and it pleased him to put in place changes where an area of desert eventually became the bed of a sea and vice versa. God's nature included a whimsical side and during the times when he was in a jovial mood he would rain down a whole plague of frogs or locusts on the earth and enjoy observing their effects on all the different species there.

Eventually, however, God came to realise that there was something missing from the world. The creatures on the earth did not do very much apart from eat, sleep, multiply and die. God received much pleasure from watching his animals, but their antics were rather limited. He wanted more action and excitement and so he called for a divine committee to consider the creation of a new type of creature that would carry out a multiplicity of different tasks and provide interest and excitement for him. Furthermore, the demands of monitoring the development of billions of planets were rather severe and he felt that with respect to earth some local help would be beneficial. A new creature could help and save him a lot of work.

To consider the matter he assembled a committee consisting of the usual archangels he used for such purposes. Each of them was divine, of course, but somehow a typo occurred in the text message sent to each participating being and the word divine was substituted by the word design. This committee thus became known as the Design Committee and somehow the name stuck. The committee met in the Divine Conference Room one Sunday morning after prayers, and when all the design members were seated and nectar and biscuits served, God outlined his demands. Then, after receiving an urgent call on his mobile, he departed, leaving his subordinates to discuss the details.

The senior design member, the Archangel Michael, folded his white wings and called the meeting to order.

'We are charged with designing a multi-purpose creature to conform to God's purposes for the planet it has pleased him to call earth. There are many aspects of this creature to consider. The main ones that need to be designed first include: structure, mobility, the ways in which the creature is fuelled and its ability to interact with its surroundings. Once we have agreed on these, we can consider more subtle matters such as its degree of intelligence, cognisance, psychological profile and so on. Are there any questions so far?'

'Yes,' replied the Archangel Raphael. 'Are there any

more biscuits please? We have no chocolate creams left at all.'

Michael called for the cherub of the biscuits and placed an order. 'Now if everybody is happy, we can get on. What size of creature will suit our requirements?'

A long discussion ensued and eventually a size smaller than a mammoth and greater than a rabbit was agreed. It was thought that a vertebrate creature with calcium as the main element for its frame would be adequate. The frame would be covered by layers of ectodermal tissue of sufficient strength to maintain the structural integrity of the animal. Contained within the ectodermal tissue and the frame would be the inner organs and multiple layers of bound, stretchable fibre which would act as strands to enable the frame to move. All this was readily agreed as it formed the basis of many creatures already present on earth. The whole creature would ideally weigh between two and four talents[1].

'Are there any more questions?' the Archangel Michael asked.

There was a long pause and eventually Gabriel spoke. 'Are there any more biscuits, please?' he asked.

Michael again called for the cherub of the biscuits and placed another order.

'Now if everybody is happy, we can get on. What about the creature's method of movement?'

---

1   Note: one talent weighs about 60-70 pounds.

A long discussion ensued again and eventually it was agreed that the creature should have four legs, one end of each of which would be split into five smaller, flexible talons. These would help it grasp and hold other materials. The committee was divided on whether a tail should be provided for balancing purposes and eventually a small stump was agreed, but this was really no more than a sop to those who thought that a tail was elegant, rather than it being believed it would serve any real purpose. Fuelling the creature's movements was again fairly simple with the preferred method of supplying the necessary energy being the partial oxidation of animal and vegetable residues. The discussion about the creature's ability to detect its surroundings took a long time with some angels favouring radar while others preferred the cheaper method of using receptors to detect the electromagnetic spectrum between the infrared and the ultraviolet regions. Any more than two receptors would have been inelegant and any fewer meant that the desirable 3-D detection would have been impossible. It was also agreed that the creature should be fitted with an olfactory system and vibration detectors throughout its surface area.

The question of species continuation was always one which embarrassed the angels. Angels themselves did not need to reproduce. If God wanted another angel he just made one, but for him to make another of their proposed creatures whenever necessary would be a great chore and so some type of species continuation process was essential.

This was an important point and after much discussion, during which the biscuits were seriously depleted, the committee agreed that a form of asexual reproduction should be introduced. The process called fragmentation was eventually decided upon. In this process a small part of the creature could be removed and if placed in a suitable culture medium it would eventually grow into a fully grown and mature creature. Having agreed on the main physical dimensions of their creation, the committee then took a comfort break, which also permitted the biscuits to be replenished. A quick lunch of ambrosia and nectar was enjoyed and then the archangels rested their wings for a short time as they were rather heavy and when they had been seated for some time the wings tended to give rise to aches in their shoulders.

After the break the intelligence of the creature was discussed. At first this gave rise to hoots of laughter. Intelligence on earth? Such a concept was novel indeed. However, after a long discussion in which it was established that intelligence was a dangerous gift to give such a creature, it was agreed to provide some measure of intelligence as an experiment, which, hopefully, would provide God with the additional amusement he craved. Since the creature was symmetrical in one direction, it was decided that an elementary form of brain should be inserted at its higher end. The latest type of simple brain – the mark ten – was suggested. This consisted of two symmetrical halves enclosed in a strong calcium-rich shell. Each half would have different functions and in a moment of rare jocularity it was decided that the left half of the brain would control the right half of the creature and vice versa. The brain would be designed and constructed with multiple linking of nerve centres, which permitted a learning process to develop. The whole job was a bit of a botch-up but in the time available the archangels could not do much better. Eventually the design of the creature was almost finished.

'Well,' said Archangel Uriel, 'thank goodness that's finished. I wonder what it looks like?'

Michael was good at drawing and quickly made a rough sketch.

'Good God!' they all exclaimed.

'Mind what you say,' said Michael quickly. Then he added: 'it does look rather comical though.' All the angels then fell about laughing.

'Look at that!' exclaimed Raphael.

'And that!' exclaimed Gabriel pointing. 'Will that really do what we expect?'

The laughter continued for some time with Gabriel continually wiping his eyes.

Then Michael, who was the most serious of the archangels, made a pertinent comment.

'We haven't thought of a name for our creature. Any suggestions?'

A number of suggestions were made, and rejected, and so Michael decided that, if he approved of their work, God himself might like to name their new creation.

Later that day God returned and inspected their work. He stared at it and pulled at his long, white beard. 'Well. It's not what I expected, but the engineering seems sound enough. It will do for that little world.'

So saying, he put his stamp of approval on it right in the centre of its belly. 'As for a name,' he continued, 'how about an Autonomous Divine Auxiliary Mock-up?'

And that is how the very first man was created.

POSTSCRIPT

After many years of watching the first man's antics and laughing uproariously every time his creature did something stupid (which was all the time), God felt that a little more tweaking would improve the situation and provide even more comic interludes. Furthermore, the first man had not increased as per the design plan. The fragmentation method of reproduction was not working very well and although the first man had long since perished there was still only a single descendant.'

God thought and thought and eventually devised a simple plan. This involved taking the sole man aside and after putting him to sleep, painlessly removing one of his ribs and around it building a similar creature. The new creature had some slight differences: a few extra lumps here and there and a different mind. God activated this new creature by blowing hot air into it, which had the effect of bringing it to life but also resulted in its emitting hot air on every possible occasion. At the same time the fragmentation process of reproduction was abandoned in favour of something even more comical and which left God in stitches of laughter. The new creature caused the man much aggravation, including enthusiastically disposing of all his wealth, and so God gave it the name, Extremely Vexatious Entity.

And that is how the very first woman was created.

2

THE MITIGATION OF GOD'S DISTRESS

And in the fullness of time there came into heaven a moment of worry.[2]

At first there was only a slight rumour but that in itself was extremely rare. Not since the days when Lucifer had been expelled from heaven had there ever been any hint of disruption, disturbance or even anything unusual in heaven, but there was no doubt that the rumour was genuine. That the rumour came from the very top of the angelic hierarchy was also not in doubt as there was no other possible source. Clearly it must have commenced in the First Choir (which consisted of the Seraphim, the Cherubim and the Thrones) and then passed through the Second Choir (which consisted of the Dominations, Virtues and Powers) and all the way down to the Third Choir (Principalities, Archangels and Angels). At first, of

---

2   A note in the celestial diary.

course, nobody took any notice, but the persistence of the rumour was such that firstly, doubts as to its authenticity were dismissed, then credulity ensued and finally belief. The essence of the rumour was that God himself was suffering from distress.

All the angels in the celestial hierarchy were worried, but the archangels and angels were worried far more than the others. This was due to the rarity of the situation and the lack of information as to the effect the rumour would have (if true, of course) on their lives. This latter fear was hardly surprising, as it is always the lowest in the pecking order of any organisation who suffer the most from the consequences of corporate trauma, and being the lowest of the third order the angels did not want to be the scapegoats. It may surprise the followers of these stories to know that within the celestial hierarchy there was no procedure for dealing with comments or complaints. On reflection, however, it will be realised that there had never been a comment or complaint and hence no procedures were necessary to deal with one.

Thus, it came about that in the absence of any such procedure the two lowest orders of angels decided to hold a meeting to discuss the situation. Archangel Michael took upon himself the responsibility for contacting the others, which he did, of course, with his mobile phone. It was a most useful and yet simple phone with only four numbers on it. Number One was the Help desk for God himself (and Michael's phone did not usually permit access to this number) and Numbers Two, Three and Four were the Help Desks for the Three Choirs in descending order of status. By dialling any one of the three permitted Help Desks, and activating the appropriate menus, Michael had electronic contact with every member of each Choir.

One day after prayers they had gathered in the heavenly garden (called inevitably, the Garden of Eden) by the statue of the Holy Mother to discuss the matter. As the senior member of the archangels, Michael folded his white wings and called the meeting to order.

'Has everyone heard the rumour that is currently circulating?' he asked.

There was silence in the Garden of Eden.

'What rumour is that?' asked Archangel Uriel, yawning. He had been fully occupied recently and being the only angel in heaven who had not heard the rumour he was puzzled by the attitude of the angels. Having slept badly the previous night he had been dozing in the meeting until he was roused by Michael's question.

'That was really a rhetorical question, Uriel,' remarked Michael a little stiffly. 'I'm surprised you haven't heard. Please pay attention.'

Uriel nodded and proceeded to fall asleep again.

'We have all heard, Michael,' said Raphael gently, 'except for Uriel, but what can we do? How can we help God?'

'I have spoken to one of the Principalities and I can confirm that they, too, are worried and are having a meeting just like ours,' replied Michael. 'In fact,' he went on, 'there are meetings going on all over heaven to discuss the matter. All Three Choirs are involved. The Second Choir is holding a huge meeting with every member of the Dominations, the Virtues and the Powers present, and I believe that The First Choir is similarly engaged – some thousands of angels.'

'Wow,' said Gabriel. 'Surely that guarantees the authenticity of the rumour?'

'True, true,' said Michael moodily and lapsed into silence. This lasted until the Archangel Uriel woke up, yawned once more and stretched his wings.

Archangel Michael was not amused. 'Wake up and please pay attention, Uriel. There is a strong rumour circulating throughout heaven concerning the fact that God is worried, and we are discussing it.'

'But,' Uriel remarked (recalling that in heaven it was occasionally permissible to start a sentence with a conjunction), 'surely the nub of the matter is what caused the rumour. That God is labouring under distress is disturbing enough but why is he disturbed?'

'We do not know,' came the answer.

'Can we find out?'

'No chance, matey.'

There the matter rested and so it was with all the other more senior meetings; nobody knew or could find out.

Heaven continued with its usual business but clearly the fact that God was worried was a concern to all the angels and everybody went around heaven with frowns as they wrestled with the problem.

A month or two passed[3] and then a development occurred. This came about through the work (unauthorised) of the angel Sariel. Sariel was, and always had been, interested in electronics. He had created his own private workshop in heaven and in his spare time he would happily tinker with the controlled flow of electrons through semiconductors, gases and vacuums. Advanced wire-less modems were also a speciality of his. After one session in his workshop when inspiration had struck him, he found that one piece of electronic wizardry he had developed gave him access to the telephone link between all the Help Desks, including God's own personal Help Desk. This was a link that was normally forbidden to Third Choir angels.

Could he resist the temptation to listen in? He wrestled with his conscience, just as Jacob had wrestled with God, and eventually reasoned that since God knew all things, he must know that Sariel had developed his piece of kit. If God did not want him to use it, then he would never have allowed Sariel to invent it in the first place. Thus, having placated his conscience, he listened to the conversations between the Second Choir angels and God. These, to his amazement and joy, revealed what the rumour was, and it was divine dynamite. He could hardly believe it, but

---

3   These were heavenly months, which are different from earth months.

he knew that his duty was to inform the archangels and angels in his Choir.

He went to the Archangel Michael, explained what he had discovered, and suggested that he, Michael, hold another meeting where more enlightened discussions could take place. This Michael did and when all the Third Choir angels had assembled again in the Garden of Eden, he folded his wings and called the meeting to order. Mainly to stop him from falling asleep again he appointed Uriel as secretary and charged him with the responsibility for taking notes on his tablet. Michael then addressed his colleagues in a shaky voice.

'I have called this meeting to announce that Angel Sariel has through supplication and electronic ingenuity discovered what the rumour is about. I am asking him to inform us of his findings. He claims to know the reason for God's distress and before I consult with the Second Choir angels, we need to know exactly what Sariel has discovered.'

'Before we start,' interrupted Archangel Raphael, 'are there any more biscuits, please?'

'No there are not,' said Michael crossly, 'but if you really must eat something there is some angel cake over there by the statue.'

Everybody, including Sariel, then helped themselves to a large slice of cake, and then after munching quickly and wiping crumbs from his mouth Sariel addressed all the angels.

'Fellow angels. In my workshop I have developed an electronic device which permits me to listen in to the telephone calls made between all the Help Desks – including' – here he paused for dramatic effect – 'those of Help Desk One.'

Uproar followed. Wings were unfolded and refolded, hands put together as if in prayer, the statue was upset and calls for mercy from God were made. To add to the disorder a thick cloud floated across the Garden of Eden and momentarily the angels could not see each other. As they scurried about trying to avoid the cloud wings became entangled with other wings and soon there was utter confusion. Eventually Archangel Michael pulled himself together and took charge.

'Stand still everybody, stand STILL.' Everybody stopped doing what they were doing and as soon as the cloud had passed some semblance of order was restored.

'You actually know the reason for God's distress?' asked a minor angel in amazement.

'Yes, I do.'

'And don't you have any fear that God disapproves of you discovering the telephonic link between the Help Desks and telling us everything you have found out?'

Then to everybody's amazement there was a sudden swirl of wind and God appeared. His face showed signs of worry but, nevertheless, he smiled.

'Do you think, angels, that I would allow Angel Sariel to invent his gadget if I disapproved?'

'No, Lord, no,' replied the angels in an unfortunate, cringing sort of way.

'Angel Sariel has my authority to inform you of *our* difficulties,' continued God, 'as they are *our* difficulties and affect everyone present in heaven.'

Then with another sudden swirl of wind God disappeared. The angels were rather shaken by this surprising appearance and called for a little light refreshment of ambrosia to calm themselves. Then, reassured that their meeting was legal and approved, Archangel Michael called for Sariel to continue with his findings.

Sariel was an extremely old angel and all this excitement was almost too much for him. He mopped his brow and sat on the remnants of the cloud until he had regained his composure. Then he resumed talking.

'As you all know, heaven is the place where everyone on earth (or, at least, all those who have lived an admirable and approved life) comes after he or she has died, for their judgement and salvation.'

The angels all nodded sagely.

'It appears,' said Sariel, perhaps a little sadly, 'that human beings have been increasing and dying at too fast a pace for heaven to cope with. In short, heaven is running out of accommodation. God's building contractors are building new mansions as fast as they can, but the pace of building is insufficient, mainly due to the lack of good building sites. There are also limited options for expansion and, I believe, the celestial green belt is now under threat.'

The angels were horrified. They had assumed that heaven was infinite and that there was room for everyone who was eligible. Apparently, this was not now the case. This was a revelation, and the meeting buzzed with the sounds of anxious and now even more worried angels. There was little chance of any order being restored for some time and so Archangel Michael closed the meeting saying that the minutes would be circulated as soon as possible.

The truth of the matter became public knowledge soon afterwards all over heaven, resulting in heaven-wide turmoil. All three Choirs then knew about the problem and God was so upset that he was seen on fewer and fewer occasions. He missed some of his usual prayer meetings and the angels wondered where he had disappeared to. The truth was that he was reclining on his favourite cloud (which was shaped like an armchair) in his inner sanctuary and thinking about problem solving in general and their housing problem in particular.

The problem was unique, and God was suddenly made aware of his inexperience in resolving it. The usual problems associated with the management of millions of ancient worlds were "a piece of cake," (a phrase he had picked up from observing human activity) but this one was completely different. After considerable cogitation he consulted his reference book about the earth. This slim volume contained all the notes that he had compiled when he had first created the earth. There he read a few thought-provoking things that had slipped his mind. He shut the book with a bang.

'I shall have to call a meeting of the First Choir angels,' he thought out loud.

This was a meeting of the highest management group he could muster and was held in the executive room on cloud nine. Unfortunately, the meeting was not a great success as the Seraphim flew round God all the time singing, 'Holy, Holy, Holy is the Lord of Hosts,' as was their wont, and the Cherubim were only slightly more helpful and could think of nothing other than the expulsion of man from Eden and the Annunciation of Christ. Soon God realised that he should consult the more practical angels, who were, of course, the archangels and angels from the Third Choir, and so another conference was arranged in the meeting room in the emergency conference room.

The angels from the Third Choir were surprised and flattered to be invited to so important a meeting and were on their best behaviour. Uriel was told by Michael that on no account was he to fall asleep and all were told to speak only when addressed by God. Each angel had ensured that his wings were in perfect condition. Best behaviour also meant that there were no requests for chocolate creams or indeed any other sort of biscuit.

God commenced the meeting with prayers and then said: 'Angels of the Third Choir, I have asked you here as you have the most experience of mortal activities and are the most practical of our celestial beings. I need to find a solution to our residence problem, but first I shall outline the reasons for it.

'The fault is mine and entirely mine,' announced God, much to the amazement of the angels. 'When I created men and women, I instilled into each one a desire to reproduce themselves. This is what I called the "urge." Its purpose was twofold: firstly, to provide entertainment for us in heaven and secondly, to allow the species to create beings in their own likeness to replace them and who would sequentially manage the earth. I did, however, make a grave mistake.'

The angels all gasped again. Such an admission from God was unheard of. He continued: 'I told the mortals: *"be ye fruitful and multiply; bring forth abundantly in the earth and multiply therein,"*[4] and they did so with commendable enthusiasm. I could wish that they had obeyed my other commandments with similar enthusiasm but this they have obstinately refused to do. Unfortunately, the "urge" I implanted was too strong and human beings have reproduced at an unimaginable rate. I planned for a rate of reproduction being a factor of X mortals/unit of time whereas the current rate has proven to be X^{100} mortals/unit of time. Now we find that the number of souls reaching heaven is far greater than my estimate. Consequently, there is now a housing shortage in heaven and I don't know where to put them all. I'm even considering doubling up the souls in each mansion, but I don't like it.'

The angels all gasped again. Wings were flapped in alarm and many called for a small chalice of nectar to

---

4   Genesis 9:7.

calm themselves. Prayers were hastily said.

'Unfortunately,' continued God, 'the mortals appear to be unable to control this "urge" and although they recognise that their world is overpopulated all their attempts to reduce their rate of reproduction have failed miserably. The thought is there but the will is not – the "urge" is still far too strong. That is, however, a secondary problem; our immediate concern is the housing problem. As the most practical of my angels, I'm asking you for any suggestions that could improve the situation.'

Part of the job description for the angels of the Third Choir included the responsibility for monitoring the mortals and protecting them from evil. The task that God had asked them to solve was right up their street and after a moment's thought they put forward several suggestions.

Archangel Michael was the first to speak. 'Could we not change the houses so that instead of great mansions they occupy terraced houses? It would mean a more effective use of the space that is available.'

This was not an unreasonable suggestion since terraced housing was common on earth.

'A good idea,' said God.

Archangel Raphael spoke next. 'Could we not extend the longevity of mortal existence? That would mean fewer souls arriving at the Pearly Gates.'

'A good idea,' said God.

Then Archangel Uriel spoke. 'Could we not decrease the power of the "urge"?'

A good idea,' said God, 'but it would be difficult to do and wouldn't help our immediate problem.'

Then Archangel Gabriel spoke up. 'Could we not somehow delay the journey to heaven so that fewer souls arrive at present?'

'A good idea,' said God.

There was a longish pause while the others who had not spoken thought and thought. Meanwhile God stroked his long beard and ruminated. 'These are all good ideas,' he said, 'and I shall ensure that they are all put into practice, but none of them would entirely solve our problem. There must be a more effective process as well.'

Suddenly there came the clearing of a celestial throat. Then a rather embarrassed minor angel rose to his feet and unfolded his wings. It was Angel Sariel, the inventor of the celestial telephone.

'Forgive me for speaking,' he said rather modestly, 'but I believe that the housing problem and the rate of mortals' souls attempting to enter heaven can be resolved by a simple reallocation of worthiness. If we raise the requirements for the worthiness of our current population of mortals' souls, then many of those who are currently located here will not meet the new standard. They can then be moved away from heaven. Similarly, the multitudes of souls who will be applying to enter heaven in the immediate and distant future will also not meet the required standard. Thus, at a stroke, the numbers will be reduced by an amount dependent upon whatever standard of worthiness is set.'

31

'A good idea,' said God. Then after a moment's thought: 'that's brilliant!' Then a disadvantage suddenly occurred to him. 'It's an excellent idea but what shall we do with all the mortals' souls that have been downgraded – er, sorry, I mean regraded?'

Angel Sariel looked embarrassed again. In fact, he looked extremely embarrassed – so much so that he was reluctant to speak.

'I do have a suggestion,' he muttered, 'but it is rather awkward for me to say.'

'Spit it out,' said God kindly, 'you are among friends.'

'Well… well…' stuttered Sariel, 'we could always send them *down there.*' He pointed vaguely to somewhere beneath his feet.

There was silence in the room. If angels had any pins and someone had dropped one, it would have sounded like a pistol shot. The silence went on and on until…

'What a brilliant idea,' said God, smiling. 'The more I think about it the more I like it. It would be warmer for them there too.'

Then with smiles and handshakes all round, the meeting was adjourned.

Thus, it came about that the problem of the housing shortage was resolved and with it, God's distress vanished. The descriptions of the worthiness of mortals' souls were adjusted and those affected were relocated[5] to another

---

5   The official term used in the celestial diary.

place.[6] It was not found necessary to downgrade the quality of the mansions in heaven and all was happiness and light. For his pains Angel Sariel was upgraded to archangel and encouraged to continue playing with his electronic bits and pieces, but for some unexplained reason his telephone link between the Third Choir angels and God's Help Desk never worked again.

And in the fullness of time the moment of worry in heaven was dissipated.[7]

---

6   Not Crosby in Lancashire.

7   A note in the celestial diary.

3

AND SAINT PETER SMILED

Saint Peter was a worried saint. The efforts of mankind in establishing a world of peace had resulted in extensive wars that proliferated and expanded rather than decreased, and the ensuing carnage had meant that many more souls than usual were all queuing up and waiting, some rather impatiently, for entrance into heaven. Of course, being of very recent human origin the souls still contained elements of their humanity and those in the queue were jostling for position and attempting to reach the head of the queue before anybody else. Arguments frequently broke out, particularly between those high officials of the various churches and religions on earth and those celebrities who considered that their lives entitled them to preferential treatment. They had, after all, enjoyed enormous privileges before they had died and considered that death was an insufficient reason for those privileges to be withdrawn. Thus, it came about that those people were bad-tempered, argumentative and weary with waiting for their processing to commence.

Not only was Saint Peter worried at the multitude of mortals' souls awaiting processing, but he was completely unable to comprehend why mankind was doing its best to destroy itself. If mankind wanted peace, and war was the consequence of its actions, why, he thought, didn't mankind apply reverse logic and actively promote conflicts? The result would surely be that peace would break out everywhere, but he believed that mortals were far too irrational for such creative thinking. His workload was, however, too great to allow him much time for such speculation and introspection. His job was to interview and assess the new souls that arrived in heaven and to judge and, if necessary, sentence them. He was worked off his feet and had to rest at frequent intervals. He occasionally sat on a dense cloud in front of a desk to conduct his business but for most of the time he found it more convenient to stand, which inevitably resulted in his feet and wings aching. As he was a senior saint, he had wings and, unless he was careful they would flap about behind him, causing his shoulders to ache even more and upset his balance. To mitigate this, he had tied his wings together using a band of light. This technique was common to many angels whose lives were spent standing up, and was effective at preventing 'wing drop' - a common problem for angels, as well as reducing the resulting discomfort.

Saint Peter had done his best to reorganise the selection procedures and make them more effective. He had introduced many tables, each with its own angel processing the applications, and this had proved to be beneficial until arguments had broken out between impatient applicants. Peter had also introduced a numbering system, similar to those used in banks, hospitals and some large retail units on earth. This system utilised a device located at the beginning of the queue. It was fitted with a narrow roll of parchment consisting of numbered tags. Each soul took a tag when he reached the beginning of the queue and only when his number was called out was his application considered. These changes had produced a big improvement in the time spent processing applicants, but there were still a few who considered themselves above such plebeian behaviour and attempted to force their way to the head of the queue. When this happened Saint Peter merely indicated to one of the two burly, grim-faced angels, who stood nearby and acted as bouncers. These were Dumah and Sumah and they were authorized to deal with any problem. Usually such behaviour led to the miscreants being given a short taste of hell which, strange to relate, often had no effect on them. The troublemakers then re-joined the queue at the end. Only that day had Saint Peter been compelled to call the bouncers over when four aggressive lads had attempted to damage the Pearly Gates.

Saint Peter was required to impose some form of judgement upon the new souls: some would be allowed to enter heaven while others were snubbed. It was not usually necessary for him to devise anything complex, as his laptop contained punishments for all and every occasion. All he had to do was to look up the offence in the file marked 'PUNISHMENTS', and the bouncers would see that it was properly implemented. Occasionally, however, and he had the authority to do this, he introduced punishments of his own devising. These were creative rather than vindictive and were imposed when he thought they were more appropriate than the recommended punishments. Someone, for example, who had eaten meat during the time of Lent might have to eat meat every day for the equivalent of a thousand earthly years or thereabouts. A thief might have to endure all his belongings stolen for a similar time. His possessions would be returned to him shortly after the termination of the punishment time and then, before he could enjoy them, they would be stolen again. Even apparently trivial matters were considered and someone who, for example, poked someone else in the eye would spend a lifetime having their own eye poked. All these punishments took the form of the guilty party suffering what they had done to someone else. More severe punishments were also imposed when necessary and the guilty party might well be led across the floor to the fire-blackened door which was the entrance to the steps leading to the underworld. The judicious application of creative justice also permitted hell to be reached by other ways, but the fire-blackened door was the one most mortals' souls feared and in their minds was associated with endless torment and agony.

Saint Peter sighed and took a sip of nectar from the sparkling glass by his side.

Number 456,396, please,' he called.

A medium-sized soul with bright yellow trousers and a pink bald head stepped forward to the table. He was the latest applicant who wished to enter heaven. Peter grimaced at the ostentatious colour of the soul's trousers, gritted his pearly white teeth and asked: 'name and heavenly number, please.'

'Joshua Slocum, matey,' replied the man, 'and I don't know what a heavenly number is.'

'It's the same as your National Insurance Number,' said Peter wearily.

'Wot's that?' said the man in the yellow trousers.

Saint Peter sighed and clicked on his laptop. 'It appears that your number is YE 33 46 78X.'

'If you say so, guv,' replied Joshua.

Peter read the entry about Joshua Slocum on his laptop and hummed and hawed. Then he tutted to himself and clicked his tongue.

''Ere, mate. Wot am I doing here?' asked Joshua, 'and what's that round thing on your head?'

Saint Peter looked at him. 'Can't you recognise a halo when you see one? Now tell me how you feel?'

'Orl rite, matey, orl rite.'

'How were you feeling a week ago?'

'Poorly, very poorly. I'm orl rite now but I've got no idea where I am.'

'You are standing outside the entrance to heaven.'

'Cor blimey, mate. Does that mean I've died? Who would have thought it?'

'Tell me, Mr Slocum. Do you consider that you've been a godly person?'

'Yes, mate. Not too dusty.'

Saint Peter looked again at the entry for Joshua Slocum on his laptop. 'Apparently you have been married four times.'

'Yus, that is correct.'

'It says here that the second, third and fourth marriages were bigamous.'

'Bigamous? Wot's 'at mean, matey?'

'It means that you were not divorced from your first wife when you married for the second, third and fourth time.'

'Couldn't see the point really. The other women left me when I took up with the Jones girl. I can't leave the ladies alone. Always been like that, matey. Here! What are them white wings on your back? What are they for? Are you going to a fancy-dress party?'

Saint Peter sighed again. 'No, Mr Slocum, I'm not going to a fancy-dress party. It also appears that you have amassed considerable wealth and material things to excess. Much of which has been purloined by you. Your attitude towards your fellow man is appalling: you have bullied and abused them. Where, Mr Slocum, is your regard for the well-being of your fellow men?'

'Look arter number one, mate. That's my motto and

always has been.' He winked at Saint Peter.

'If everyone did that, Mr Slocum, then who would look after those people who are unable to look after themselves?'

'That's the job of the council, me old china.'

'I see.' Saint Peter read some data on his laptop and then leaned back, thought for a moment, looked Joshua Slocum directly in the face and said: 'by the powers invested in me after my ascent into heaven I have the privilege of being your judge and jury.'

'Judge and jury?' said a surprised Joshua Slocum. 'Wot for? I ain't done nuffink wrong. Wot are you judging me about?'

'Your life, Mr Slocum, your life. Your life has not accorded with the recommendations of our Lord. I see that you have transgressed almost every one of the Ten Commandments and have amassed considerable brownie points in the Code of Conduct for earth which you will know as the Seven Deadly Sins. Your sins are, however, of much less importance than one other matter for which there must be a considerable punishment and I have no alternative than to send you to a place of learning – we do not always refer to it as a place of correction even though there is a variable and considerable element of punishment involved. There you will eventually receive instructions as to how you can learn from the experiences of your last life. Many aeons hence you may be able to re-apply for consideration for your entrance into heaven. I'm giving you a pamphlet that contains advice about this process.'

Saint Peter gave him a sheet of paper and indicated to one of the bouncers. 'Please follow the guide there and he will show you where to go.'

'Wot's this other matter wot's so bad then?'

'You can't even guess?' asked Saint Peter. 'It is, of course, those appalling trousers you are wearing. The colour is a sartorial sin of great magnitude – an abomination in the eyes of the Lord and, indeed, everyone else in heaven.'

'Heaven? I don't believe in heaven. Where are you sending me?'

'Then how can you go to a place you don't believe in? No, you are not going to heaven. Thank you for your application. Good luck.'

Saint Peter beckoned to one of the burly grim-faced angels who, as he approached, flexed his muscles.

'Come with me, please, sir.'

Joshua Slocum objected to being told what to do but was somehow unable to prevent his feet from taking steps towards the fire-blackened door. A wisp of black smoke curled round the door and a sort of muffled roaring could be heard. The grim-faced angel opened the door and showed Mr Slocum the steps leading down. His last words were: 'Cor blimey! Wot's all this then?' Looking rather apprehensive he took a few tentative steps down and then the door closed behind him.

Saint Peter sighed and looked at his list again.

'Number 456,450, please,' he called.

The soul of an extremely fat man waddled up to the table. His face must once have been handsome but was now distorted by rolls of fat and a great hanging jowl similar to the dewlap seen in cattle. He looked well-dressed, as his tailor had most effectively managed to disguise his gross stomach and thick legs that resembled tree trunks. From the quality of his clothes and the number of sparkling rings on his fingers, it was apparent that his wealth was considerable.

'Name and number please?' asked Saint Peter.

'I'm Sir Edward Pellew, a man of substance and importance. What number do you want, my man?'

'I can see you're a man of substance,' said Peter dryly. 'I need your National Insurance Number, please.'

'GX 28 45 11S. Is that what you need?'

'It is. Now tell me why you are so fat, Mr Pellew.'

'That is an extremely rude question, and be so kind as to address me with my proper title. It is SIR Edward Pellew. I would have thought that my size is an indication of my worth to society. To succeed in life is the object of our existence and my size indicates that I have succeeded and am a highly regarded citizen. I'm aware that I have passed over and have no doubt that I shall be permitted to enter some heaven and live as a spirit of authority in the way I have become accustomed to.' He sniffed.

Saint Peter turned to his laptop and read some files.

'I see, I see,' he muttered to himself and stroked his beard while he thought. He turned his attention back to Sir

Edward Pellew and regarded him for a moment.

Pellew was not amused. 'Why are you regarding me in the way that a headmaster looks at a recalcitrant schoolboy?' he asked sharply, 'and who are you anyway? If it comes to that, where am I? This doesn't look like heaven to me. Answer me, please.'

Peter smiled. 'I understand that material wealth is regarded as a sign of a successful person almost anywhere on earth. On whose authority do *you* base this definition of success?'

'It is axiomatic, it is a worldwide definition and it is obvious, of course. Why would you doubt it? How else would you decide and measure success except by the acquisition of wealth? But I will remind you that you haven't yet told me who you are and by what authority you are questioning me.'

'My name is Peter,' answered the saint. 'Bishop Peter if you require a title, and I'm here to judge your life and take appropriate action as to your future.'

'On whose authority do you presume to take this action?' asked Sir Edward sharply. 'I'm not accustomed to being told what to do and am perfectly capable of deciding things for myself. I will remind you that you haven't yet answered my second question.'

'I judge you on the authority invested in me by God.'

'God? God? Which God is that?' asked Sir Edward. Then before Saint Peter had a chance to reply he continued: 'the only God that I recognise is that of Mammon.'

'I can see that is so,' replied Peter sadly. 'I also see that having died you presume that the status you achieved on earth will continue in heaven. Tell me, Sir Edward, what do you think about people who, often through no fault of their own, do not achieve wealth or indeed eminence in any field?'

'I got where I am through hard work and damned hard work at that. I wanted to live in luxury, to eat the finest foods and drink fine wine and enjoy the good things in life. High living is available to anyone with the talent and the drive to succeed. If people don't want to live in comfort, then that is their choice.'

He paused for thought and then burst out angrily: 'I detect a hint of disapproval in your voice. How dare you presume to judge me?'

'What I do is done with the authority of God,' thundered Saint Peter. 'I will quote a parable from the Bible: The Book of Saint Matthew, Chapter 19, Verse 24, where Jesus Christ says: "it is easier for a camel to go through the eye of a needle than for a rich man to enter the Kingdom of God."' He took a deep breath and thundered at Pellew: 'do you think only of yourself? Have you no concern for those less fortunate? You have been given many privileges and yet you have soundly abused them. You are an ill-principled man. You are guilty of hubris and selfishness. How can you expect to enter heaven?'

Pellew stared at Saint Peter in astonishment and started to reply but Peter thundered at him again: 'you are a far greater failure than those you have scorned, and you will endure a punishment commensurate with that failure.'

Pellew snarled and started to get up but one of the burly angels stood up and approached with a look of determination on his face.

'Sit down and listen to me,' bellowed Saint Peter. 'Do you know the story of King Sisyphus?'

'I do not,' replied Pellew angrily. 'I want...'

'Be quiet and listen to me,' interrupted the saint. 'You are the camel in the parable of the rich man. Your life has been a wasted life of self-indulgence and personal abuse, and you cannot enter heaven until your soul has been purged of your pride. Punishment for those who disobey the word of God is within my power and takes many forms. You, Sir Edward Pellew, will suffer the ordeal of King Sisyphus but your stone will be the need to consume the choicest and richest foods until your appetite has been satisfied and then, and only then, will you know that your hunger has not been assuaged.'

'That sounds fair enough to me,' said Sir Pellew who was puzzled and surprised at the way he was being treated. He did not understand why he was being punished, but it appeared the punishment wasn't a punishment at all. It was to be a continuation of the life he had enjoyed on earth. Perhaps it was a reward. He was delighted with the way events had turned out.

'How long do I have to endure this "punishment"?' he asked, smiling broadly.

'Until the end of time,' replied Saint Peter shortly. He turned to the burly angel standing beside them.

'Dumah! Give this man a Bible and take him to the place I have spoken of.'

Thus, it came about that Sir Edward Pellew spent eternity doing the things he had enjoyed most when he had been alive.

'It is an interesting observation, Dumah,' remarked Saint Peter, 'that the mortals view hell only as it was described by their poet Dante – all fire, horns and agony. They are incapable of realising that hell takes many forms and is invariably a place of their own making.'

Dumah inclined his head before returning to his post.

And Saint Peter sighed.

After a moment of contemplation, Saint Peter turned again towards the queue of waiting souls.

'Next, please. Number 456,893.'

The soul of a little old lady bent from the extreme curvature of her spine came forward. Her clothes were so ragged and dirty it was clear that she took no care or pride in her appearance. She was so bent over that little could be seen of her face, but what small part was visible looked as though it hadn't been washed for weeks. She carried a small bag to which she clung with such force as suggested it contained something of great value to her. She did not look directly at Saint Peter but turned her face away and looked downwards. As a mark of respect, she attempted to curtsy, but her disability prevented her from achieving any degree of elegance.

'Who are you?' the saint asked. 'Please give me your name and National Insurance Number.'

'Morning, your Lordship,' she muttered, looking anywhere except at Peter. 'My name is Rebekah Cornwallis. I'm a poor old widow woman whose husband has deserted me, leaving me penniless.'

'Do you know your National Insurance Number, Rebekah?'

'Nah, your Lordship.'

'It matters little, but your number on earth is equally valid when in heaven.'

'Is my bus pass valid as well?'

Saint Peter smiled. 'There is no need for buses here, Rebekah. Tell me where you think you are?'

She peered about her in a furtive manner. To Rebekah it appeared that she was in an immense celestial room with nebulous walls. Close by were two or three portals, the largest of which was some form of gate made from shimmering light. There were other portals with an assortment of phrases carved in the lintels over them. What their purpose was, Rebekah had no idea. At some distance away was a cramped, ancient and heavily barred door from which some wisps of an evil-smelling black smoke emanated. Occasionally this door was opened to permit some soul to enter and some cramped steps could just be seen leading down into a pit lit by flickering red flames. Most of the souls who stepped through this portal were trembling but just occasionally one would be joyous.

Behind her, Rebekah saw the long queue of souls, chattering and arguing as they attempted to push their way to the head of the queue to be judged. This queue stretched out so far into the distance that its end could not be seen.

In front of her Rebekah saw the tables. There was an angel with its wings neatly folded, resting on a small dense cloud behind each table. Each angel was questioning a soul. There was nothing on the tables except a chalice containing some nectar, a laptop and a small mobile telephone. Standing near the angels were the two grim-faced muscular angels. They were as still as statues until they were needed.

'Dunno, me Lord,' she said. 'It don't look like heaven to me but then it don't look like hell either.'

Saint Peter looked at her. 'You are in neither of those places, Rebekah. You are in the Great Hall of Judgement where recent arrivals are interviewed and decisions made about their future.'

Rebekah looked even more furtive and her eyes slid away.

'I ain't done nuffink wrong,' she muttered.

'Tell me what you have done with your life,' asked Peter, reading something on his laptop.

'I ain't done nuffink wrong,' she muttered again.

'Tell me more.'

Rebekah stood there with her head hanging down

saying nothing. Eventually she muttered: 'what you gonna do with me?'

'Well, if you won't tell me I shall have to tell you a little about your life. You have spent your whole life considering your own interests. You were very young when you married and your reason for marrying was to find someone who would look after you. You then ignored the needs of your husband and your children and cheated and lied for the rest of your life. You were given talents when you were born but have steadfastly refused to develop them. You are slothful and impatient of others. You have gratified your desire for alcohol until it has killed you. What do **you** think I should do with you?'

'It weren't my fault, sir. Them children were always fighting and crying. My husband was a …'

'I know all about any extenuating circumstances, too,' interrupted Saint Peter. He looked at the little bag she was clinging to as though it was a precious possession. 'What have you brought with you in the bag?'

'Nuffink, me Lord – just a trinket.'

'Open the bag and show me what's inside.'

She opened the bag. Inside there was nothing at all.

'Do you know what was inside your bag, Rebekah?' asked the saint.

'No, sir,' she muttered miserably.

'Inside were hopes; the hopes and aspirations of your life. Well, Rebekah, what shall I do with you? Shall I send you down the steps over there into hell?'

'NO SIR, NO SIR,' she screamed. 'Anything but that. I'll be good next time, your worship. I promise.'

Saint Peter thought for a moment and then said: 'Rebekah Cornwallis, look at me. LOOK AT ME. You will not be entering heaven, nor will you go to hell.'

'Thank you, my Lordship. Thank you.'

'Instead, you will go to the saloon numbered 101 and there you will learn everything that you need in order to live a just and honest life. Then, and only then, will we know what to do with you.'

'Yes, sir.'

Saint Peter beckoned to Sumah. 'Take this soul to saloon 101.'

Sumah took Rebekah Cornwallis by the arm and helped her over to one of the portals. She passed through the two swinging doors. Over the portal and unseen by Rebekah was a notice. It read;

ROOM 101 – THE LAST CHANCE SALOON

And Saint Peter sighed.

'Number 456,921, please.' Peter was looking at his laptop and didn't see the soul of the next applicant until he was standing right in front of him. The man was short and dressed exactly as a bishop. He wore a long cope ornately embroidered in scarlet and gold, joined at the chest by a beautifully worked clasp. On his head was a mitre. He also wore a small gold cross and carried a highly ornate golden crozier.

'Ah, bishop. I see you are dressed in your finest vestments.' Saint Peter was always pleased to see any man of God, but rarely did they appear in their full regalia.

The bishop looked at the glorious Pearly Gates shimmering in beautiful light. This, he thought, is where I belong.

'Thank you, sir. Yes, I deemed it appropriate to my status to appear in my finest clothes.'

Saint Peter looked carefully at the entry on his laptop. 'Bishop... bishop... bishop. I can't seem to find you here, bishop.'

'Surely an oversight, sir,' replied the bishop. 'I am the Bishop of Marton in Cheshire and my National Health Number is LD 13 45 89X.'

'Thank you. Yes, yes, here you are, I have you now.' Saint Peter smiled at the bishop. 'These computers are always giving us trouble – in heaven, as it is on earth – you may have spoken those words before or, at least, something similar. I shall have to consult Archangel Sariel again. He knows about computers and things and I really don't know what we would do without him.'

He read the entry about the bishop and sighed. 'Tell me about your life, bishop. What do you regard as your successes and what do you regard as your failures?'

The bishop had been looking forward to this. 'Well, my Lord. By the way, is that the correct form of address to you?'

'It will serve,' replied Saint Peter.

'Well, my Lord, I have believed in the existence of God all my life. I can never remember a time when my belief has been challenged and from the time I first enjoyed cogent and intelligent thought I felt God calling to me and I wanted to say yes. The only way I knew of achieving this ambition was to become a member of the church. I desperately wanted to serve and consequently I spent many hours on my knees praying for this to happen. I was not ashamed to speak my mind on the matter when all my school friends entertained doubts as to the existence of God, and consequently I frequently suffered verbal abuse. I took no notice but resolved to become a cleric as soon as possible and at the earliest opportunity I enrolled as a novice in an ordination college and thence…'

Saint Peter interrupted him. 'No, I don't mean the route whereby you became ordained and appointed a bishop – I know all about that. What I want to know is what you did with your life after you had been ordained.'

'Yes, my Lord. Through prayer and devotion, I soon gained an admirable reputation and rose rapidly through the ranks until I achieved a bishopric. My success was due in part to the quality of my sermons for which I won many prizes. These came to the attention of the BBC and soon I was asked to take part in religious debates. I became famous for my speeches and for the quality of my sartorial elegance.'

On his cloud Peter started to squirm at this litany of boastfulness but said nothing.

The bishop continued without pause. It was almost as though he was reading a prepared speech in readiness for his being offered some religious prize.

'I have devoted some of my time to spreading the word of God to the proletariat and I have enjoyed every minute. More importantly, I have been intimately involved in many ecclesiastical matters of great significance associated with Chester Cathedral and have enjoyed the company of, and intercourse with, archbishops and high officials of other religions including (here he paused for dramatic effect) the Holy Father in Rome, and the rich and famous of many countries. It has been my privilege to dine with politicians and academics of all persuasions with whom (here he visibly preened himself) I have had considerable influence and gained an enviable reputation. Not a bad record, I believe. Success has followed me wherever I have gone.'

Saint Peter had been tapping his fingers on the table in considerable irritation at this speech. 'And your failures? What of them?'

'My Lord, it is hardly for me to say but I am unaware of any failure.'

'I see.' Peter stroked his beard and stared at the bishop. 'Tell me please, bishop, if you were going to enter Jerusalem, how would you travel?'

What an odd question, thought the bishop, but however odd it appeared it required an answer.

'I would fly to Ben Gurion airport and then take a taxi.'

'Hmm. Have you ever concerned yourself with the

poorest people in society or those in need of comfort, solace and help?'

'My Lord,' replied the bishop. 'Matters pertaining to the proletariat are the concern of the ordinary vicars and priests. My strengths lie with the senior clergy.'

Saint Peter leant back on his cloud and regarded the bishop carefully. After a long silence he spoke: 'Bishop, you must be aware that you have committed some of the Seven Deadly Sins…'

'WHAT!' interrupted the bishop. 'Impossible! God has always been at the centre of my life and…'

'STOP!' shouted Saint Peter, and in his agitation his halo slipped to one side. 'You know nothing about God. Did Jesus boast about his achievements? Was he filled with pride? Did he strive to achieve high status by associating with the high and the mighty? Of course he didn't. He associated with the poor and the needy, NOT the rich and influential, and if you claim to follow the life of Christ you must do the same.'

He paused for a moment and then continued: 'you know nothing about the matters in which you claim to be an expert, and are uninterested in the matters you confess you know nothing about. You are a man who professes to be a Christian but have acted as though Christianity was unknown to you. By the powers that God has invested in me I sentence you to enduring an eternity of washing the feet of the humblest people on earth. You will know humility. You will know what it is to wear rags. You will know what it is to beg for your food, to beg for your life, to struggle to achieve even the simplest of things and to endure physical and emotional pain. Then, and only then, can you possibly become a Christian.'

He turned to his angel. 'Dumah! Give this man a Bible, escort him to room 101 and strip him of his finery.'

Saint Peter's last words were: 'Bishop! Before anything else you will read the Bible from cover to cover.'

The astonished bishop was led off and once again Saint Peter sighed.

He turned again to face the queue. It stretched far into the distance.

'Numbers 496,567 and 496,568, please.'

An unlikely-looking couple walked slowly forward. The first was the soul of a rather tired-looking woman. The problems of life were etched on her face and yet she smiled and talked to a small girl whose hand she was holding. The child was weeping and asking for her mother. Peter was upset to see them.

'Who are you, please?' he asked kindly.

'Please sir, I am Thomasina Featherstone and this child is Phyllis Smith.'

'Let me see.' Saint Peter consulted his laptop again and instantly all the details about Thomasina and Phyllis' life were displayed before him.

'I want my mummy and my dolly,' cried Phyllis.

'We have lots of dollies here,' said Saint Peter. 'What was yours called, Phyllis?'

'My favourite dolly was Amanda but what I really wanted was the beautiful dolly I saw in the shop window, but she went to my friend, Jenny. Jenny's daddy is very rich, and she gets everything she wants. It isn't fair.'

'No, Phyllis. You are quite right. Life is not fair but that is because everyone is different and has different needs. The purpose of life on earth is to learn one or more lessons, just as in school, but each person has to learn different lessons.'

He looked at Thomasina. 'What are your National Insurance Numbers, please?'

'Mine is GY 46 56 67P but I have no idea what Phyllis' is.'

'No matter, I have it here somewhere if only I could get this computer to work properly. You are associated with Phyllis by the occasion of your passing over[8].

'Yes, it was so sad. My heart bled for Phyllis' mother. Please tell me, sir, where are we and what are doing here?'

'Those shimmering lights,' replied Saint Peter, pointing, 'are what on earth are called The Pearly Gates. They constitute the entrance to heaven. Before any soul is admitted he or she has first to come before me, or one of my team, for an appraisal of their life. Depending upon the result the soul is then either retrained, punished or permitted to enter heaven.'

'But... but,' stuttered Thomasina, 'I'm an atheist. My experiences in life have led me to believe that God cannot exist.'

---

8 Here Saint Peter was being tactful in using the phrase "passing over."

'If God doesn't exist then where are you now?' the saint asked.

'I don't know,' the atheist replied miserably.

Saint Peter looked at his laptop and took a long time in carefully reading and rereading the files relating to the two souls in front of him. While this was going on Thomasina was talking gently to Phyllis and pointing out the beautiful shimmering gates beside them. Gradually Phyllis grew calmer and started to look around her with renewed interest.

'Tell me about your life, please, Thomasina. Tell me why you have spent almost the whole of your life helping others.'

'From my youngest days I wanted to be a doctor and help eradicate diseases and cure my fellow men and women. I was lucky in that I was able to succeed and for a few years I worked in a hospital. Then one day I realised that my time and energies could be better spent helping the people in some of the poorest countries in the world. This need grew on me until I decided to join a medical group helping people who were the victims of colossal calamities such as earthquakes, widespread flooding or even drought-induced starvation. I stayed with them for twenty years working in different places. Latterly I worked with Phyllis' parents who were missionaries in Africa. My work finished when the village we were working in was attacked by tribesmen who objected to "western" beliefs, as they called them, and even the aid they received. My last memory is that of the tribesmen firing guns at us.'

'Explain to me why you do not believe in God.'

'It's simple really. Why does a God who, it is claimed, is both omnipotent and benevolent, permit the horrors that pervade our world? I have seen humans suffering from the effects of excessive greed of politicians and violence from the military, whose object is only to enhance their own wealth and influence. In effect they are working to become gods themselves. Oh, it makes me so angry. Why doesn't God stop all this? He has the power but not, apparently, the inclination.'

'God's plan for the earth is beyond your understanding, Thomasina,' Saint Peter immediately replied. 'All he asks of his people is that they act in the way that he, through his son, Jesus Christ, taught them. Soon all will become clear to you but meanwhile here are five reasons why suffering is so prevalent. One, it is a repentance – a call to turn from treasuring anything above God; two, it is reliance – a call to trust God and not the people and artefacts on earth; three; it is righteousness – suffering is the discipline of God so that we come to share his holiness and righteousness; four, it is a reward – the greater the suffering on earth the greater will be the reward in heaven; five, it is a reminder – that God sent his own son into the world to suffer, and he overcame the agony.'

Saint Peter closed his laptop and looked benignly at the two souls before him. Then a beautiful angel appeared and sat down beside the woman and the child. Phyllis looked at the angel and smiled. 'You are just like my mummy,' she said.

The angel took her hand. 'Will you let me be your mummy now?'

'Yes, please,' cried the child.

The angel smiled and linked arms with Thomasina Featherstone and all three walked through the Pearly Gates into heaven.

And Saint Peter smiled.

4

THE STATUS QUO

In heaven as it is on earth God has commanded that:

Six days thou shalt work, but on the seventh day thou shall rest.[9]

In heaven, however, unlike on earth, Sunday is a day of work. The angels all worked for six days of the week but for one day they were instructed to rest. As there were no such things as earth-type days in heaven, the periods of rest were not specified in advance but allocated by God himself according to his humour and whim. Thus, in periods of intense activity there were few days of rest but at other more convenient times rest was taken and enjoyed. The angels all had their own fancies, hobbies and pleasures which they indulged in with relish when formal work was forbidden. A tolling bell, which was used only for these purposes, announced the commencement and termination of the rest periods. Its toll was deliberately unique so that there could be no confusion with other bells.

---

9   Exodus 20:9-10.

To a new soul who had recently entered heaven, the activities of the angels on a rest day were seen, in some ways, to be surprisingly similar to those on earth. Why should that not be so when the Bible records that men and women were made in the image of God?[10] On looking about him a new soul might well see a group of angels practising their singing, others would be reading ancient texts or transcribing the Dead Sea Scrolls and comparing them with the original events that prompted the scrolls to be written. Some would be paying attention to their personal appearance by preening their wings and polishing their halos. Others would be indulging in the construction of devices. Archangel Sariel, for example, would undoubtedly be beavering away in his electronic workshop trying to understand the erratic movement of electrons in the advanced modems he was devising. A number of new and interesting devices for the benefit of all in heaven had been discovered by him in this way.

The less practical and intellectual of the angels might well be seen playing games comparable with those on earth. The sports that are the subjects of many of mankind's pleasures were, with one exception, unknown in heaven for the obvious reason that having no physical body makes physical activities rather difficult. The angels might occasionally watch a football match on their television screens but since they were unable to play the game

---

10   Genesis 1:26.

themselves there was little serious interest. The whole point of kicking an inflated ball of plastic around for ninety minutes was entirely lost on them. They regarded all sports in the way that a dog would regard a smelly rubber ball. It was the same with all other physical sports, and running was regarded as just plain comical. In fact, all athletics were regarded as a quaint whim that humans suffered from; it was a defect that arose from the inconvenience of having a physical body.

The exception was quoits. The angels loved to play this game and used a spare halo which had been straightened out and placed in a vertical position as a stick, and their own halos as rings to throw at it. The game ended when the shimmering stick was full of shining halos.

The earthly games that were intellectual rather than physical were popular, however, but Monopoly and bridge particularly so. Monopoly was much appreciated and although it had originated on earth, the angels had adapted it to suit themselves.[11]

The game of bridge was another of those games invented by humans and deemed to be worthwhile playing in heaven because of its ability to intellectually challenge the players. It was extremely popular and on rest days many tables of bridge could be seen in progress. To add to the excitement a bridge league had been formed in which teams from each of the Three Choirs of angels competed.

---

11   See the Mitigation of God's Wrath.

The angels used playing cards which were similar in meaning to the earthly ones but very different in appearance. They did not use the four earthly suits of clubs, diamonds, hearts and spades; instead each suit was labelled with the name of a type of angel from each of the Three Choirs. There was a minor suit named Principalities, from the Third Choir, which was the earthly equivalent of clubs; a second minor suit called Dominations, from the Second Choir, which were the earthly equivalent of diamonds, and two major suits: Seraphim from the First Choir, which were the equivalent of hearts and finally Gods, which were the equivalent of spades. The ascending order of the suits reflected the ascending order of the levels of the angels, with the highest and most valuable suit reflecting God himself. No trumps were the same as on earth. It was a popular game with seven Gods vulnerable (and making) being second only to seven no trumps vulnerable as the most valuable contract. God was irked that seven no trumps was a higher contract than seven Gods, and it was something he fully intended to rectify one day. The scoring was the same as on earth except that blessings were used instead of points with Imperial Match Blessings being the equivalent of Imperial Match Points.

On one rest day when the bridge tables were fully occupied, four archangels from the Third Choir were engrossed in their game. The Archangels Michael and Gabriel were pitted against the formidable talents of a crack pair of angels who were the Third Choir champions.

These were the Archangels Raphael and Uriel whose competence was so great and their winning was so frequent that it was regarded as the status quo.

The four were playing rubber bridge; Michael and Gabriel were suffering from a particularly bad run of cards and were losing by two rubbers to nil. Not only that but their overall score (which formed the basis of the three-rubber match) was lamentable. Blasphemy was, of course, strictly prohibited, but when Gabriel had picked up five hands in succession with fewer than four blessings, he was sorely tried. Instead of uttering a profanity (which would have meant a penalty amounting to the loss of the game and hence the match) he called for some of his favourite custard creams to alleviate his irritation.

'I've had almost no blessings at all,' he complained to no one in particular and everyone in general. 'I don't seem to have picked up a highly ranked Domination or a Seraphim for ages. All I get is cherubs.[12] It's enough to try the patience of a saint.'

'Never mind,' said Michael with sympathy. 'It's only a game.'

'People only say that when they are losing,' replied Gabriel huffily.

The game continued with Michael and Gabriel continuing to pick up poor cards. The etiquette of the game did not permit any gloating or even a smile of satisfaction,

---

12   A cherub was a non-court card.

but their angelic nature did allow their opponents to enjoy the good hands. Any satisfaction had to be kept to themselves and although Raphael and Uriel went to considerable pains to hide their good fortune, Uriel had great difficulty in keeping a straight face, and in his efforts not to smile his mouth twisted in a lop-sided sort of way. The first two deals of the third rubber again went to the winning pair. They made two Gods with an overtrick for a score of sixty blessings below the line and thirty above and then a contract of two Principalities for a score of forty, thus giving them one hundred blessings below the line. This amounted to them having made the first game of the third rubber and left them vulnerable. All they needed was a single game call for them to win the match with an enormous score.

It was Archangel Michael's turn to shuffle and deal the cards and this time he took special care, all the while offering a short prayer for good luck. Whether his prayer was answered, or good luck prevailed, cannot be determined, but the cards that Gabriel picked up seemed at first glance to consist of nothing but court cards. Every card had a picture on it. He looked at his hand in disbelief as he saw almost nothing but aces and kings and just one or two cherubs.

The other angels saw Gabriel's mouth drop open with surprise. His wings flapped again as though he was agitated, but for the opposite reason than before, and the others knew that he must have an extremely strong hand.

'Holy Mother!' he exclaimed.

'Watch what you say, please,' said Michael sternly, 'after two passes it's your turn to open the bidding.'

'Four no trumps,' said Gabriel hoarsely. He could hardly keep the excitement out of his voice.

His partner knew he was asking for aces and replied: 'Five Principalities.'

'Five no trumps,' asked Gabriel.

'Six Dominations,' replied Michael.

'Seven no trumps,' announced Gabriel triumphantly. The satisfaction in his voice was evident.

'Doubled,' intervened Uriel.

'Redoubled.' Gabriel could hardly get his bid out quickly enough.

Seven no trumps doubled and redoubled was a colossal score of plus two thousand, two hundred and forty blessings and one which, if the contract was made, would mean that Michael and Gabriel would just win the match. The status quo would be shattered at last.

Gabriel wanted to enjoy the moment when his opponents would be defeated for the first time in ages and he hesitated for a moment after the opening lead had been made and Michael had spread his hand as dummy.

'Good luck, partner,' Michael said.

Gabriel was just about to call for a card from dummy, after the opening lead had been made, when Michael's mobile tinkled out a tune recognisable as a Bach cantata. From the precise tune Michael knew that God wished to speak to him.

'Excuse me, please,' he politely said to the others. 'This must be important.'

He listened and went pale.

'Yes, my Lord,' he said after a long pause. 'At once, my Lord.'

He put his phone away. 'I'm sorry, my friends but I have to attend a meeting with God at once. Something has happened which requires the immediate attention of the senior management of heaven.'

He turned to Gabriel: 'I'm extremely sorry but the game cannot be completed. This matter is extremely urgent. It looks as though you will be unable to play the hand and that means Raphael and Uriel win again. Very sorry, partner.'

He unfolded his wings and flew away, leaving Gabriel silently fuming. A ferocious look appeared on his angelic face. 'Now, of all times,' he muttered.

Once again Raphael and Uriel were hard put to hide their pleasure and amusement at the outcome of the game and their mouths became twisted again in an agony of trying not to laugh.

'Just remember,' remarked Uriel, perhaps a little unkindly, 'that it's only a game.'

Gabriel's patience was as sorely tried by these events as they had ever been before, and he stormed off to find a small and an exceptionally soft cloud to sit on while he ruminated about his unfortunate luck.

It was considerably later when Archangel Michael returned and immediately called for a meeting of all the

Third Choir archangels and angels. His face was as black as the ace of Gods and the others knew that something important was about to be disclosed. The assembled angels were not surprised since despite the earthly opinion that everything was sweetness and light in heaven, the contrary was the truth and either problems arose with irritating frequency or unexpected things kept happening.

When everyone was seated, Michael addressed the meeting.

'Archangels and angels of the Third Choir,' he started. 'I have news to impart which is the most important that I have ever been required to communicate to you.'

The other angels were immediately apprehensive, as Michael did not usually speak in this ultra-formal way unless he was shaken to his very core.

'I have been informed by God himself that a personal meeting has been requested between himself and another angel.'

The angels were puzzled. This was not that rare an announcement.

'Are we permitted to know who this audacious angel is?' asked Raphael.

'You may,' replied Michael. 'It is none other than Lucifer, or Satan as he is often called. You will recall that Lucifer is the angel whom I fought long ago to rid heaven of his presence. Apparently, he has asked God if he can be re-admitted to heaven.'

To say that uproar ensued would be to understate

the impact this announcement had on the angels. Hosts of feathered wings were flapped in agitation and uncontrollable gasps of amazement were heard from all. Many fell off the clouds they were sitting on, which led to considerable anguish and disturbance. Three angels who were least seriously affected merely opened and shut their mouths, rather like goldfish (had there been any, of course). Gobsmacked is a rather coarse term to be applied to angels but it described their reactions very well. All, without exception, prayed for guidance and deliverance from evil.

Knowing the sort of reaction that would follow his announcement, Michael had arranged for jugs of holy water to be supplied and the angels all immediately took a long drink and dampened their fevered brows. Some also used the water to dampen their wings in an attempt to reduce the uncontrollable fluttering that was inevitable. After some time, when the angels who had suffered most had recovered, some semblance of order was restored.

'What?'

'Why?'

'How?'

'When?'

'I have told you all I know at present,' replied Archangel Michael. 'I understand that God is now engaged in serious contemplation, which means, of course, that an immediate rejection is not being considered.'

Once more the angels could hardly believe their ears.

Were Satan's proposals really being taken seriously? Archangel Michael allowed a considerable amount of time for the assembled angels to absorb the information he had provided and settle down. Then he spoke again.

'Angels of the Third Choir. Listen to me. You all know that Satan is the personification of all evil, but I suspect that you know little else about him. God has, therefore, authorized me to give you a résumé of Satan's life in heaven. You know that God created the heavens and the earth and all forms of life. It follows that God must also have created Satan but how, I immediately hear you ask, could God have created an evil entity? The answer is that he didn't. Originally Satan was not an evil entity. He was an angel with the name of Lucifer which meant "morning star." Lucifer was an angel created by God and fashioned to rule over the earthly kingdom of Tyre. He was created a perfect and divine being, an angel of great beauty and wisdom, and one who held the highest rank in the angelic hierarchy. However, he soon became so impressed with his own perfection that he began to desire for himself the honour and glory that were rightly God's. Eventually he decided that he was of greater importance than God himself and this led to a conflict with God which ultimately became a battle between good and evil. We fought against him and his supporters and we won, and Lucifer was eventually cast out of heaven.[13] With his followers – Beelzebub and

---

13   Revelation 12:7-9.

the other deluded angels who had supported him – Lucifer set up his own kingdom. This is an illegal kingdom where he and all the evil spirits and demons who had supported him in his endeavour to overthrow God reside. It is called the underworld or hell. His name was changed to Satan and he became the highest authority of all the angels who have been cast out of heaven.

'Since then Satan has tempted angels and non-angelic species, such as mortals, to worship him. His followers, the fallen angels, are demonic and all hold out seductive promises to their victims which are not kept. There is a parallel here on earth when just before a General Election, politicians will make promises which they know cannot be kept.

'This is the being who has contacted God with a request to be readmitted to heaven. You are all required to pray for God and also for Satan in the hope that he is sincere in his wish to change the status quo and to turn over a new leaf.'

Depressed, dismayed and apprehensive, each angel departed to his private accommodation and for the next few days nothing was heard but their prayers and supplications.

Meanwhile God was considering the matter. He had never tolerated any demonstration against his authority and had acted as judge and jury in all matters of indiscipline. There was no question of this changing now. He stroked his beard and ruminated, as was his wont in times of crisis. How was he to deal with this request from Satan?

Could he be trusted? He doubted that, but if Satan was not serious in his wish for reformation what was the point of requesting a return to heaven? God's mercy was infinite, which demanded that he must consider the proposal, but what if it was merely a ruse to augment Satan's own authority and challenge God's supremacy. If this was so, then God's wrath would be terrible to witness, and his vengeance would be commensurate with the crime. He thought and thought and eventually an idea came to him. He immediately phoned Archangel Sariel and asked him to come over at once.

When Sariel arrived, God outlined his plan and asked him whether he could carry out his wishes. Sariel was honoured and delighted to help.

'It's no trouble at all, my Lord,' he said. 'What you want can be knocked up within a few days. I take it that you want complete camouflage?'

'Of course,' replied God.

'How long will you require the device to operate for?'

'That's difficult to say. It should be capable of being sustained for a few earthly days at the most.'

'And you think that the Garden of Eden will be suitable?'

'I do. It is a peaceful place which is consistent with the objectives of the meeting and it holds a particular memory for Lucifer.'

'Fine, fine, my Lord. There is no better place.'

'Then let it be so,' replied God.

જી

It would be incorrect to say that the following time in heaven was free from anxiety. Except for God, and perhaps Archangel Sariel, every angel, saint and cherub was frightened rigid.

Only once before in those terrible days when Archangel Michael had been forced to engage in battle with Lucifer had evil been present in heaven itself and, as Michael himself put it: 'I cannot but feel extreme fear when I realise that Lucifer will be here again.'

God himself had, of course, no fear of defeat. Nevertheless, with all the other matters which were occupying his mind, he had little stomach for this one.

Shortly afterwards Archangel Sariel reported to God that the device was ready and all he required were the coordinates for the meeting place in the Garden of Eden. When these were provided, Sariel sent them off to Satan in a text message with a covering note outlining the date and the time for his meeting with God, and a reminder that Satan must come alone. A brief acknowledgement was received in the form of a thumb's up emoji.

The time arrived for Satan to put in an appearance. It had been necessary for God to adjust the security settings on heaven's intruder-alarm systems. Had he not done so then the mere approach of Satan would have automatically activated the alarms with strident bells and clanging noises which alerted the residents of heaven to take appropriate action to eject the intruder. As it was, Satan was permitted to enter the precincts of the Garden of Eden without any alarm becoming activated. It was expected that his entry would be typical of fallen angels: he would appear in a puff of foul-smelling smoke.

Few of the angels present knew in exactly what form he would appear. Some thought that he would appear as a muscle-bound superman in red garb with horns projecting from the top of his head; others thought that he would appear out of a wall of fire, with bloodshot eyes and holding a trident; yet again others thought that he would assume the form of a snake, but nobody really knew.

Archangel Sariel had been put in charge of communications and he had arranged for the whole interview to be recorded and broadcast on giant screens all over heaven. This was so that everyone who had not been invited, or had lost their ticket, could see and hear everything that was being said.

The precise location for the meeting was in the Garden of Eden in an arbour just beside the Abbey Fountain. It was a place of unimaginable beauty and deemed ideal for a discussion about a peace proposal.

With the exception of God, all of the occupants of heaven were clustered round the giant screens waiting for some demonstration of Satan's power: a blast of thunder perhaps, or a sheet of fire which would announce his arrival. Instead at the appointed time, a charming melody played on a flute was heard and then suddenly the diminutive figure of an extremely attractive female angel appeared. She folded her wings neatly, sat down on one of the clouds provided, crossed her legs and waited patiently.

'Is that Satan?' asked Uriel. He and some of the other archangels were sitting close to one of the giant screens and the surprise in his voice was clear.

'Don't be fooled by appearances,' replied Michael. 'Satan can take any form he wishes. Of course, it is him. No other entity from hell is authorized to be present today.'

Silence reigned in the Garden of Eden and then a nightingale started to sing his beautiful song and at the same time God appeared. He sat on a similar cloud to Satan's but raised slightly higher.

There was no formal introduction, none was necessary – and the two looked at each other.

'This is a delightful place, my Lord,' said Satan. 'It is even more beautiful than I remember.'

'I recall with great clarity the last time you were here,' replied God. 'You had taken the form of a snake and had just persuaded Eve to eat fruit from the "tree of the knowledge of good and evil." You knew that this was forbidden. You said to Eve that this would make Adam and Eve aware of the differences between good and evil. You did all this despite knowing that you would be punished for disobeying my laws. It was intended that your punishment would be to crawl upon your belly like a snake for ever after and be the enemy of mankind. Adam and Eve had disobeyed my commands as well and were banned from the Garden of Eden and subsequently knew what pain and suffering were. You were responsible for all this. What do you say?'

'My Lord. You are right.'

'Then,' continued God, 'you attempted to usurp my authority in all matters. You gathered susceptible entities and corrupted their minds. You attempted to overthrow my authority and fought against the will of heaven. For all this you and your foul colleagues were thrown out of heaven into the place of torment and punishment we call hell. There you have continued to undermine my authority in my creations. You have worked tirelessly to promote evil whenever and wherever you can. You have placed temptation before the creatures I have created; and for the price of their souls, you made promises that conflicted with my demands. On what do you base your request for a change in the status quo? Why do you now come to me?'

'My Lord,' replied Satan. 'I have done all those things. I am guilty of everything you have said. I stand accused and plead guilty. Yet I am weary of this continued battle for souls and seek forgiveness.'

So saying, Satan knelt before God who stroked his long white beard and quizzically regarded the kneeling figure before him.

'In the past you have been unequivocally associated with untruths, trickery and all that exemplifies evil. How can I believe that you are now of a sincere mind?'

In the space allocated to the archangels, Michael and

his colleagues were watching the interview on a huge, coloured screen.

'Well said, God,' muttered Gabriel. 'Don't believe a word she says.'

'My Lord,' replied Satan. 'In my defence I would say that you created the world and all that is contained therein. You created me and hence my potential sins must have been known at the time of my creation. Are then not my sins also your sins?'

'Sneaky,' said Raphael from his position by the giant screen.

God's face darkened at Satan's comments. 'Do you not understand the concept of original sin? Do you not know that every one of my creatures is born with sin as part of its being? You, of all my angels, should have known that the capacity to sin is within us all.'

'Then why, my Lord, do you condemn me for doing that which I was born with?'

'I cannot believe that you ask that question. It is by *overcoming* sin that my creatures gain in spirituality. The way to perfection in heaven is to rage against sin and to overcome it. You have embraced and enhanced your sinful activities rather than overcome them. Your sins are far greater than those of my other creatures and your punishment will be appropriate and commensurate. Your weariness of sin is insufficient reason to permit you to enter heaven.'

Then Lucifer's face changed from a smile to a grimace.

'Then your answer is to forbid me to enter heaven?'

'I have no alternative.'

By the giant screens the angels all breathed a sigh of relief.

Satan looked at God and as she did so her face became distorted with rage.

'In time I will overcome your reluctance,' she snarled. 'In time I will become the god of heaven. Already I am collecting souls at a rate faster than they are queuing up to enter heaven. All I have to do is to wait and eventually heaven will be mine.'

She looked round at the paradise which was the Garden of Eden. 'If this is paradise and it can't be mine now then it will belong to no one.'

She waved a hand and immediately a wind sighed as it passed through the Garden of Eden. Then the screams like those of a banshee were heard, and sheets of flame appeared in many places. The trees, bushes and plants began to burn and soon the whole of the Garden of Eden was ablaze.

The angels looked horrified at the carnage. They could hardly believe what they were seeing, and many had their hands over their faces to cover their distress.

God just sat there unmoved. 'You have just failed my test,' he said to Satan. 'I needed proof of your sincerity and your actions have shown this to be non-existent. Go back to your hell.'

Satan's face twisted with rage and she changed into a

demon. A wisp of black smoke emerged from her mouth and lightning crackled all around her. She stood up and raised both her hands as if to bring down some curse upon God but before she could speak God raised his right hand.

'GO,' he commanded in voice of thunder.

Satan immediately disappeared, and God still sat there immobile while the Garden of Eden burned all around him.

To the watching angels it seemed as if God was unmoved. To Archangel Michael though, it appeared as though a slight smile could be seen on God's face, but he couldn't be certain. They all watched as God remained there for a moment or two and then he was gone and all that could be heard was the crackling of the vegetation as the Garden of Eden burned to a cinder. Soon all the screens showed was a land of dust and ashes.

After a short time, God called for another meeting with the Third Choir angels.

'Archangels and angels. I have already spoken to the other angels. Tell me your opinions of that encounter.'

As the senior angel Michael naturally spoke first. He addressed the whole room.

'Let us praise the Lord at our deliverance from evil. Let us pray.'

All the angels bent their heads and prayed.

'My Lord,' continued Michael when the prayers had been completed. 'Our relief at the unmasking of the devil is evident. We regret, however, the loss of the Garden of

Eden and are puzzled by some of the comments about sin.'

God smiled. 'Come with me,' he commanded. The angels all followed him to the place where the Garden of Eden used to be.

'What do you see?' asked God.

The angels looked and looked and could hardly believe their eyes. There before them lay the Garden of Eden as unspoilt and beautiful as it always had been.

Then God turned to Archangel Sariel. 'Explain, please Sariel.'

'Angels,' said Sariel. 'Before a place for the meeting with Satan was decided upon, God was aware of the possibility that, should Satan not get his way, destruction might be visited upon the meeting place. For historical reasons God wanted the meeting to be in the Garden of Eden and he asked me if I could prepare an electronic reproduction that was identical to the garden in every way but situated in a completely different area of space. I sent Satan the coordinates of the new Garden of Eden and he accepted them as genuine. He could hardly do otherwise as the likeness was total. I was able to do all this without much difficulty and the rest, as they say, is history. Satan destroyed the fake Garden of Eden leaving our beloved paradise unaffected.'

'Well done, Archangel Sariel,' said God. 'We thank you.'

They returned to their meeting room and when all were

seated again on their clouds Raphael asked: 'My Lord, can you tell us why original sin is necessary? Why do you not abolish it entirely with all of hell and its creatures as well?'

God stroked his beard again.

'Tell me, Raphael, what do you understand by the term "high"?'

'It means, sir, that something is above something else.'

'Yes, and "hot"? What do mortals understand by that word?'

'I'm not sure, my Lord but I think it means that something is at a higher temperature than something else.'

'That is correct. What these two words – "high" and "hot" – and many similar words imply is that a comparison is being made. The concept of "high" includes the concept of "low"; and the concept of "hot" includes the concept of "cold." Within their meaning these words include their precise opposite. It must be so. If everything was at the same level then the words "high" and "low" would have no meaning; similarly, with temperature, if everything was at the same temperature then words like "hot" and "cold" would have no meaning.

'It is the same with the word "sin." If I had created a paradise where no evil at all existed, then it would not be possible to distinguish between different degrees of goodness. In other words, we can only recognise "goodness" by making a comparison with "evil." Evil is necessary for us to recognise goodness.

'Original sin is a concept that I introduced after Adam

and Eve had disobeyed my command not to eat the forbidden fruit in the Garden of Eden. Since then every human being that has been born has been born sinful; that is, original sin is a condition of birth.

'Furthermore, the creatures that I have created would have no incentive to do anything creative if they existed in a state of paradise: there would be no need. I created "sin" so that goodness and its different degrees could be identified and recognised. Without sin, there can be no progress.

'Furthermore, it is all the qualities of aggression, which we normally associate with evil, that provide an incentive for my creatures to become spiritual beings. Physical and spiritual life are just a progression to becoming perfect.'

'Thank you, my Lord,' answered Michael. 'We are delighted that the issue has been satisfactorily resolved.'

'It has,' said God. 'The status quo is unchanged.'

He turned to go and then thought about another matter.

'Archangel Gabriel, if you resume your game of bridge at the same table, I think you will find that your hand is just as it was when you left it.'

'Thank you, my Lord,' said Gabriel, smiling.

5
SIMPLE JOE

'There's summat queer going on up Eden Hill,' said Joe in his strong Cheshire accent.

That evening we had met at our usual Wednesday evening venue, the Rose and Crown pub in the village, and Joe's comment abruptly stopped the conversation about football. Joe was a character: he was a simple man with simple tastes and interests and yet, unlike the rest of us, he was deeply religious. He was honest and forthright, and his forthrightness stemmed from some inner strength and religious conviction which the rest of us lacked. Being young we were also outspoken and direct, but our forthrightness came rather from the confidence and conviction of youth, and whereas our confidence would decrease as we got older, Joe's would always remain. Joe was a farm worker and rather bovine in character, almost as though his contact with farm animals had rubbed off on him, and after spending so much time in the presence of cattle, he had gradually assumed some of their characteristics.

'Something queer on Eden Hill, Joe?' I asked.

'Yep, there were that, Tom,' he answered.

'Well, I was walking there yesterday, and I saw nothing unusual,' I remarked. 'It was as beautiful as always.'

We live in a rural village; not only is it rural but it is surrounded by some of the most beautiful countryside in the whole of England. The lake at the bottom of Eden Hill is surrounded by lush, verdant growth and the trees and bushes that encircle the lake and clothe the hill produce a picture that is quite remarkable. It is almost as though they have been planted with the sole objective of creating the most attractive picture imaginable. Even someone as talented as Capability Brown could not have created a more pleasing landscape.

'Well, there is now,' said Joe truculently.

'Tell us what happened, Joe,' I asked gently.

Joe cleared his throat. 'Another pint would help.'

This was supplied and then he started. 'Well, I were there this arternoon looking for one of my cows that had got out. I walked up the footpath to the top of t'hill, but I were only halfway when suddenly I found that I couldn't walk any farther. Then I 'ad a dream.'

'A dream?' said George. 'You! Had you been drinking, mate?'

'Nah, I 'adn't. I were as sober as a judge.'

'Judges are renowned for their drinking, Joe,' said Henry mischievously.

'What was your dream, then?' I asked.

'I saw feathers, lots of big feathers and people wearing 'em.'

'People wearing feathers up Eden Hill?' I asked in some confusion. 'Are you sure that was what you saw?'

'Yep. Feathers. Big 'uns too.'

We all looked at each other. This sounded very odd. The hill and the whole of the surrounding area were part of a conservation area and no development was permitted, so whatever Joe saw couldn't have been due to any commercial venture.

'So, what were these feathers you dreamed about, Joe?' asked George. 'Are you sure that someone hasn't started a free-range chicken farm?'

'I think,' said Henry, 'that what Joe means by a dream is a vision. It is obvious that he wasn't asleep, not at least when he was walking.'

'It has been known,' said George sagely.

Joe was indignant at this. 'I were not asleep an' you were reet, 'enry. It were a vision. That's what it were.'

'Can you recall anything else about your vision, Joe?' I asked.

'Nah, just them big feathers.'

'Ostriches or emus perhaps? Fancy dreaming about ostriches!'

We discussed the matter for some time, but Joe wouldn't admit to remembering any more. The feathers had made a big impression on him to the exclusion of everything else, provided, of course, that there was a something else. We agreed that the difference between a vision and a dream merely reflected the state of wakefulness of the dreamer and that dreaming would probably last for longer than a vision and be forgotten quicker, but we couldn't be completely certain. That Joe was serious was not in doubt; he wasn't the sort of person to joke in that way. He clearly believed that he had had a vision and we felt compelled to believe him.

Of course, we couldn't leave the matter there and we agreed to go to Eden Hill the next day and see for ourselves whether there was anything to back up Joe's allegations. He was working on his farm and couldn't join us but in the late morning Henry, George and I took the footpath that led to Eden Hill.

On the way I asked the others, 'Why is this hill called Eden Hill? It certainly seems an appropriate name for such a beautiful place, but I don't really know.'

None of them really knew why and George sensibly remarked that since it had always been called by that name, he had never questioned it. It is true that familiarity does not usually breed questioning and we had all known Eden Hill all our lives.

It was a very hot day and as we sauntered along the oak-tree-lined avenue that led to the hill itself, we were grateful for the shade.

'I'm beginning to think that walking up the hill was not a good idea,' said Henry, sweating profusely, and we all agreed that it did seem to be much hotter than usual.

The avenue petered out and degenerated into a much smaller path that led to the hill proper; this gradually made its winding way up the hill. Eden Hill was a big hill and magnificent views could be obtained from its summit. It would take us a good two hours to reach the wood at the top and as we struggled upwards, I began to agree thoroughly with Henry – it was too hot, far too hot for walking.

'Let's stop for a moment,' I gasped and without waiting for the others threw myself down for a rest. The others did the same. We remained there for fifteen minutes and then rather ungraciously, I must say, started to trudge upwards again. The hill rose steeply and as we struggled up we were soon puffing to get our breath again. As we walked it seemed to get even hotter and the urge to turn back began to grow on us.

'Has anyone brought any water?' gasped Henry. 'I must have a drink.'

'Not me,' we replied, kicking ourselves for not thinking of bringing anything to drink. After half an hour it was clear that it was just too hot to be climbing up such a steep path. We began to stumble over small rocks and tufts of grass and tempers were frayed.

'I think I've had enough,' I panted, having just stubbed my toe.

'But we're not even halfway yet. We can't give up now.' George was fitter than Henry and me.

'I'm also in favour of going back and trying another day,' said Henry.

George was in favour of continuing, but Henry and I were adamant that it was too taxing. All our energy had drained away and we sat on the grass gasping for breath like three old men in distress; and we were only in our twenties. Eventually I suggested: 'George, you continue and see whatever you can. Henry and I are knackered. We'll wait here for you.'

George agreed and he continued walking energetically up the steep path. Five minutes later he returned.

'You fellows are quite right,' he spluttered, while drawing great gulps of air into his lungs. 'It is *far* too hot.'

'Did you see anything unusual?'

When George had got his breath back, he spoke. 'No, nothing out of the ordinary at all.'

We silently made our way down the path and when we were near the bottom George said. 'It seemed to get even hotter as I went up the path. I'm sure that down here is cooler.'

'I think you mean not as hot,' I replied, 'it's certainly very hot just here.'

Slowly, like three frail pensioners, we tottered back along the oak-lined avenue and staggered into the Rose and Crown.

'Six pints of your best, landlord,' shouted George as we collapsed into one of the wooden settles that the pub offered as seats. When we had recovered sufficiently to reconsider our adventure, a thought suddenly struck Henry.

'Do you chaps remember exactly what Joe said yesterday?'

'He had a dream about feathers, big feathers and he claimed that was evidence of something fishy on Eden Hill.'

'Actually, what he said was that he had got halfway up the hill when he could go no further and then had his dream. Well, we tried but got no further than halfway either. Isn't that rather odd?'

Henry was right; none of us had realised that this particular aspect of our experience had been the same as Joe's.

'Did any of us have a vision?' I asked.

Nobody had, but the coincidence of being unable to go any further than Joe was certainly odd.

'It must be just a coincidence.'

'There is, of course, another explanation,' said Henry. 'It is well known that Joe is a simple man. His intellectual capacity is, let me say, rather restricted. Of course, he is a well-meaning and likeable chap and all that but even so with his imagination…'

His voice tailed off. There was nothing more to say on that matter. Henry might be right or there again he might not. There we left it and agreed to talk about it further with Joe the next time we met.

Later that evening we met in the Rose and Crown again and Joe was as voluble as ever. He still maintained that his experience was real and that his vision was as vivid as reality. He was surprised that none of us had experienced a vision.

'Youm didn't feel anything?' he asked. 'Nuthin' at all?' His eyebrows shot up.

We all said no, all we felt was extreme heat. It was just too hot and we had decided it would be sensible to try again another day.

'Chickens!' said Joe. 'That's what you be. You be a lot of old hens.'

Then George had an idea. 'I say, chaps. I suggest that the next time we all go we take Joe with us and we shall see if anything happens to him again.'

So that was what we decided to do.

It was a week before we were able to go up Eden Hill with Joe, and in the intervening seven days the village was full of rumours. Nobody else had managed to reach the top, but most had reached about halfway and a few reported having visions, some of which included people wearing lots of feathers. Clearly Joe's vision was the same, which was significant. George, Henry and I were embarrassed that we had doubted his story and apologised profusely and to our pleasure he took our apologies in his stride.

It should be stated that nobody had ever actually *seen* anything: the accounts of feathered people were only visions they had experienced. No other details were given. It was a mystery and we were determined to find out more.

We set off better provided this time and had brought with us plenty of water and some chocolate, which Joe carried in a backpack. As we walked through the avenue of oak trees the atmosphere did seem to be different. It was difficult to describe it, but it felt fragile, almost as though our presence was expected, which was nonsense, of course.

'I don't like this much,' said George. 'It seems a bit spooky.'

'Chicken!' was Joe's sole comment.

Henry and I also felt the same "atmosphere", but Joe seemed completely unaware of anything unusual.

'Don't be so soft,' he growled. 'There's nowt 'ere but us.'

When we came to the bottom of the path that led up Eden Hill, we saw that some heavy black clouds were coming our way. Ignoring them, we started to climb and as we climbed so the blackness of the clouds became more intense and soon rain was falling. The previous time we had been there the weather had been extremely hot; this time the rain started to fall and the higher we got the greater was the rainfall.

'Why the hell didn't we bring raincoats with us?' I shouted as water dripped through my thin shirt.

'The forecast said it would be dry all day,' Henry shouted back. 'There was no apparent need for macs.'

'Don't be so soft,' Joe growled. 'A drop o' water won't hurt thee.'

Despite the rain we resolved to continue climbing and as we got higher and higher the water began falling much more heavily until it was torrential. Soon we were all soaked through and once we were sopping wet there seemed little point in turning back. After all we couldn't get any wetter.

At last soaked, tired and irritated at the weather we reached the halfway point. This was the place where we had got to before. Suddenly a bolt of lightning lit up the dark sky and a second later peals of thunder almost deafened us.

We stopped to consider the situation.

'What's the point in continuing?' shouted George, his voice barely audible above the lashing rain and the thunder. 'I can't go much further in all this.' Streams of rain were gushing down the path like small rivers. 'I certainly don't need these,' he shouted, throwing away the bottles of water he had brought with him.

Henry and I were soaked through and had no wish to continue either. I turned to ask Joe his opinion and to my amazement saw him striding up the path. The silly, simple man! He too was soaked but apparently oblivious to his sodden clothes. I could just hear his walking boots splashing through the rivers of water that were flooding down. There was something else as well. I might have been wrong, but in between the torrential rain and the thunder I thought I could detect the sounds of the hymn "Onward Christian Soldiers."

'Look at him – the fool,' I shouted. 'Stop him. He's singing as well.'

The rest of us attempted to follow him but he was far

stronger than us, and we very soon gave up. Then another flash of lightning lit up the whole side of the hill, quickly followed by more thunder. A wind started to blow and quickly became so strong that we were in danger of being blown over.

'Come back, Joe,' we shouted. 'We're going down. Come back.'

He took no notice, even if he had heard our shouting above the howling wind and driving rain, and continued to stride up the path until he disappeared from our sight. He didn't look back once. It was almost as though some force was propelling him upwards regardless of whether he wanted to go or not.

There was no proper place to shelter on that part of Eden Hill in such a storm and having pointlessly shouted some more, we staggered and tripped our way down the hill and eventually found some shelter under the oak trees. We were all tired and gasping for breath and the relief was palpable. Strangely the amount of water that was then falling seemed appreciably less than when we were half-way up the hill, and we assumed that the storm was blowing over. We limped all the way back to our homes, dried ourselves and changed into clean, dry clothing. That was how our second attempt to solve the mystery of Eden Hill ended.

We had no idea what had happened to Joe. It was possible that he had suffered some calamity and was lying down exposed to that raging storm. We felt guilty at leaving him but then, we reasoned, he had left us, not us him. We wondered whether we should alert a mountain rescue team, but Joe was a sturdy man used to country ways and was perfectly capable of looking after himself. That evening when the storm had completely abated, we met in the Rose and Crown to discuss what to do and to our surprise and delight there was Joe sitting in a corner enjoying a pint of bitter. He looked slightly bewildered and was apparently sucking his pint down with relief.

'Joe!' we all shouted. 'How ARE you?'

'Aye, lads,' he said and took a large draught of beer.

We congratulated him on his safe return and discussed the odd storm.

'It is almost,' said Henry, 'as if the heat and the storm was deliberately trying to stop us from reaching the top of the hill. Each time we climbed it the weather was extreme, and the higher we went the worse it became. I know that sounds ridiculous but that's what happened.'

'True, true,' answered George. 'I hadn't looked at it like that. I don't think I've ever been outside in such a violent storm before. It was awful.'

We all agreed and discussed the strange weather, all that is except for Joe. He remained silent. So much so that eventually we were forced to ask him.

'Joe, what happened to you?'

'Don't want to talk about it.'

We knew him of old and were perfectly aware that after three more pints he would tell us everything, so we waited and talked about this and that. Three pints later he had relaxed sufficiently to want to talk. The effect of another pint did the trick.

'You do realise, Joe,' said I, 'that we almost sent an alert to the mountain rescue to find you. We would have done so as well if you had not appeared by tomorrow morning.'

'God were with me,' he replied. There was a strange, faraway, wistful look on his face.

'God?' we asked. 'Was he at the top of Eden Hill?'

'No, not God, but listen and I'll tell 'ee all.'

We settled down, pleased that our curiosity would be satisfied at last.

'When we reached that part of t' hill where we stopped, and it were a bit damp I felt a bit queer. It were as though my mind were sleeping and I started to imagine things. I could see them feathers again in my mind and I wanted to find out more. So, when yer shouted to go down, I went up t' hill further. It were a big struggle and got more difficult the further I went. At last I could get no further and stopped and sheltered behind that big rock, yer know. My mind was full of cloudy dreams of people and feathers. In my dream there weren't any rain at all. That were queer, weren't it? Then as I watched, my dream cleared and I saw everything as clear as I'm seeing youm.

'I saw angels, lots of 'em, but four were just before me, sitting at a table. They seemed to be playing some game. There were a board on table and counters on t' board. I heard one say: "two hundred blessings for me for passing go, Michael."

'"You always have the luck, Uriel," sayeth the one called Michael. "What property will youm buy?"'

'"I's thinking of an 'otel on Cathedral Square," sayeth the one called Uriel.

'All of a sudden I knew what they were doing. They were playing that game called Monotony, but it were a heavenly version.'

'Do you mean Monopoly?' asked George.

'Aye, that's reet, lad.'

''Do you mean to say that you saw angels playing Monopoly?'

'Youm reet there, that's what they were doing. I'm certain that be reet. But other angels were playing other games. I saw hoopla. Some were using their halos to play hoopla. There were a game of netball going on with two halos as baskets for and a thick, round cloud for t' ball. Others were reading great scrolls of some paper, some were scribing on sheets of paper, and many was playing harps and singing the praises of the Lord. Lots of 'em were looking at the view from top o' hill and I 'eard one sayeth: "T' view from top o' t' hill is magnificent. It's just like t' Garden of Eden."

'"That's why t' hill is called Eden Hill, matey," sayeth another.

'"Tis a grand place for a vaction," sayeth the first 'un.

'"Aye, lad," sayeth another angel and folded his wings. "Jus' another day here and then back to work."

'Then they all stood in a great ring and said prayers to

the greatness o' God. My dream then sort of went and I were still soaking wet behind my rock. So, I made my way down t' hill but you had all agone afore me.'

I could see from the expressions on my friends' faces that they, like me, had listened to this account in disbelief. Silence greeted the end of Joe's tale.

'Do you mean to claim that your vision was of a group of angels relaxing on a vacation, ON EARTH?' asked Henry.

'That's it, lad,' said Joe, cheerfully and burped. 'Whose round is it now?'

'Angels on holiday?' asked George. His eyes opened wide and his mouth fell open. It was not a pretty sight.

'That's it, lad,' said Joe, again. He grinned at us. 'Them angels were having a good time. Trouble with you lads is that you don't believe in such things.'

'It is a little hard to believe,' I said.

'But why should they come to earth when they have the Garden of Eden?' asked Henry, attempting to inject some logic into the story.

'Why not?' T' hill is a fair place to be. Some people on earth go abroad for a holiday when they could have the same or better at home. It be the change they want.'

'Do you believe you saw angels on vacation, Joe?' asked George.

'I do that, lad.'

George and I were stunned by these thoughts and nothing was said for a moment as we grappled with the idea.

Henry was also thinking hard. 'So, do we believe that

the difficulties in our getting to the top of Eden Hill were because the angels had so arranged for "natural events" to prevent us?'

'It must be so,' I said, 'and I understand that nobody else has managed it either – it isn't just us. Something else has just occurred to me as well. If Joe is right and that angels are enjoying a vacation on Eden Hill and that it is almost ended, then we should be able to go there very soon without any difficulties.'

'Youm be reet there, lad,' said Joe. 'Youm be reet.'

The following day we, and Joe, tried again to reach the top of Eden Hill. It might have been a coincidence, but we managed it without any difficulty. The weather was fine and nothing disturbed our progress. We looked around at the gorgeous view but saw nothing unusual. Everything was as beautiful as ever. The angels had not left any sign of habitation behind them and no rubbish, as you would expect. We looked at the view for a long time and then returned the way we came.

Was Joe's vision true? It was difficult to decide, but when I went to church (for the first time ever) on Sunday I saw Joe, Henry and George all sitting together in a pew. So, perhaps Joe wasn't so simple after all.

It was a week later that a family having a picnic at the top of the hill found something odd. Hidden behind a dense bush was the largest feather that had ever been seen. There was just the one and ornithologists were completely unable to identify the type of bird it must have come from.

6

THE PATRON SAINT

At the entrance to heaven Saint Peter was about to interview a new soul. Shane Grimshaw had recently arrived and to his surprise – for he was unaware that he had passed over – he found himself in a large room surrounded by shimmering walls. At various places in the walls were doorways of differing construction. They varied from beautiful ornate Pearly Gates that emanated a feeling of peace and welcome to one great, black, solid door, the very sight of which instilled a feeling of terror into all those who gazed at it.

Immediately in front of Shane was a bearded man sitting at a desk and writing in a large ledger. He looked authoritative and resolute and wore a halo at a jaunty angle. When he saw Shane, he smiled.

'Shane Grimshaw. Peace be with you.'

'Thank you, sir. I am sorry to say that I have no idea who you are or even where I am.'

'You are in the Great Hall of Judgement which is the entrance to heaven and my name is Saint Peter. Some people call me Bishop Peter.'

'Good heavens!' exclaimed Shane. 'I'm in heaven? Then I've passed over.'

'Yes indeed. You stand before me for your assessment of fitness.'

'Assessment of fitness? I never realised that we were all assessed at the entrance to heaven. I previously thought that any process of assessment was automatic.'

'To a certain extent you are right,' replied Saint Peter, 'but things change all the time and we are interested in your response to the new situation you find yourself in and any recent details that you may be unaware of. This is particularly true in your case as I suspect that you do not know that a proposal has been made on earth about your status and I can inform you that it will be fully implemented as soon as possible.'

'A proposal? About me?' asked Shane. 'What on earth can that be?'

Saint Peter looked benignly at Shane. 'I'm pleased to say that the appropriate authorities on earth have agreed to initiate the processes which will lead to your being designated a saint. I'm also happy to inform you that this process will proceed without hindrance and within the present earthly year you will be officially recognised as a saint. Congratulations.'

'Me! A saint! Good gracious! Saint Shane Grimshaw? That sounds rather bizarre.'

The new saint was visibly surprised. When he had recovered from the shock, he asked the first question that came into his mind: 'do I get to wear a halo like yours?'

'You will be measured for your halo when it is deemed appropriate. As I said you are not a saint yet, the award will be made later when you have been assessed.'

'Why do you have to assess me further? I ask purely out of curiosity.'

'Ah. You may be regarded as a saint according to earthly criteria but those criteria are not the same as heavenly ones and I need to decide whereabouts in our company of saints you should be placed.'

'Different criteria? I don't understand.'

'Let me explain,' said Saint Peter. 'Aeons ago canonization (which is the earthly process of declaring a mortal a saint) was almost an ad hoc process levied by people whose religious beliefs were sometimes dubious and occasionally non-existent. Once, many years ago in Sweden, for example, an inebriated monk was canonized after being killed in a drunken brawl. There have been many other cases where canonization has been inappropriate. We get all sorts here. That brings the Society of Saints into disrepute and will not be tolerated. On earth nowadays there are more rigorous procedures for admission into sainthood but due to the vagaries of mortal authority and politically inspired canonization the authorities in heaven have decreed that each new saint who arrives here is reassessed. In your case there is no doubt that your earthly qualifications are adequate. However, we still have to decide where in the Society of Saints you will fit.'

Saint Shane was intrigued by this comment. 'You make it sound as though there is a hierarchy of saints in heaven, sir,' he said.

'You may call me Peter or Saint Peter, not sir, which is an earthly title unrecognised in heaven. You have understood me correctly. There is a hierarchy of saints in heaven, in the same way that there is a hierarchy of angels. Heaven is a hierarchy just as mankind has organised itself along hierarchical lines, though I must say that the hierarchies on earth are invariably not based on spiritual criteria but on more secular and base concepts. A few religious sects have attempted to organise themselves on more spiritual lines but with disappointing results. Don't you agree?'

'Well yes I suppose so, but I understood that all men are equal in the eyes of the Lord,' said Shane. 'I can appreciate that there must be a God who is Lord of all things but how can there be hierarchies when all souls are equal?'

'All souls *are* equal, but they are at different levels of spiritual development. Mankind is learning and it is only by doing things incorrectly that he learns what not to do and hence what he should do. He forms tribes, or groups, and regards those outside his tribe as a threat. Each tribe is organised on a hierarchical basis, but the criteria of the hierarchy are invariably related to the acquisition and implementation of power. That is clear, but tell me what prompted you to spend your life caring for the weak, the poor and the disadvantaged?'

Saint Shane frowned. 'I can't explain my motives

logically. All I know is that I did what I felt was necessary to save and preserve lives.'

'Even to the extent of eventually losing your own life?'

'I've worked among the poor for years. It taught me much about myself as well as others. A job needed to be done and I wanted to do it. I didn't know then that it would end as it did.'

'Would that have made a difference?'

Shane thought for a moment. 'No.'

'Would you describe your work as a lost cause?'

'Not at first, but it soon became clear that complete success would not be forthcoming.'

'Yet you continued to do good work. What you felt was the spiritual nature of your life dominating the material side,' said Saint Peter.

'Spiritual nature? I didn't go to church very much, Saint Peter, but I often felt the need for spiritual comfort.'

'The lack of attending church matters but little. It's actions that matter, not appearances or the adoption of shibboleths or conformance to religious practises.[14] Your worship was in your work.'

He stood up and beckoned to Shane. 'Come. Let me show you the Saints' Village.'

They walked through the Pearly Gates and found themselves in a stony and ill-kept garden.

'Is this the Garden of Eden?' asked Shane. 'It's not as beautiful as I thought it would be.'

---

14   James 2:14 and 17.

'No, no. This is merely the working area for the saints and cherubs. The Cherubs' Village is also near here. This garden is not really a garden at all. It's called the Garden of Gethsemane in memory of the garden on earth where Jesus was betrayed. It is an exact copy of the garden at the time of Christ.'

As they walked Saint Peter continued: 'you are new here so I must tell you that the saints are divided into three categories. These are Level One – Impassion, Level Two – Passion, and Level Three – Compassion. Compassion is the highest level.'

'Why is that?' asked Shane.

'As I explained, the honour of sainthood as bestowed by mortals is variable, and so heaven has decreed that the saints should be allocated different degrees of seniority here. On earth there are few differences between Impassion, Passion and Compassion but here there are many. The differences govern what work is carried out by the saints.'

'If I am a saint then I will work to what end?'

'All the entities in heaven work towards their own spiritual advancement. Your work will follow this route... Whoo there!' suddenly shouted Saint Peter and ducked as a group of angels flew past, nearly knocking them over.

Shane too, stumbled and almost fell.

'Careless,' muttered Peter ruefully, 'careless. Sometimes angels are so engrossed in what they are doing that they forget themselves.'

They walked on along a weed-strewn path towards a woman whose cloak was bulging as though she had something hidden underneath it.

'Who is that?' asked Shane.

'She is Saint Elizabeth of Hungary.' He stopped, smiled and addressed the saint. 'What have you got under your cloak, Elizabeth?'

'A bunch of red and white roses for a poor widow woman, Peter,' she replied.

'May I see?'

She also smiled and opened her cloak to reveal a basket of bread.

'Ahh,' said Saint Peter, 'should I have expected anything else? God be with you, Elizabeth.'

To Shane he remarked: 'Elizabeth is an Impassion Level Saint and her patronage relates to bakers and beggars.'

They strolled on towards a clean-shaven man praying by a small pond full of frogs.

'Who is that devout soul?' asked Shane.

'That is Saint Anthony of Padua,' replied Peter.

They waited until the man had finished his orisons and then Shane was introduced to him.

'Anthony holds the patronage of those who have lost items,' said Saint Peter.

'I see,' remarked Saint Anthony, 'that you have divined the reason for my prayers just now. I have lost my book of psalms which I use for teaching. I have misplaced it and can't find it anywhere.'

Suddenly the frogs in the pond started to croak loudly and Anthony put a hand to his head as though a thought had just occurred to him.

'Ah. My prayers have been answered – I have just remembered.'

'Verily the miracles continue,' said Saint Peter and once again he chuckled. 'God be with you, Anthony. Come Shane, we have work to do.'

'Praise be to God,' replied the forgetful saint.

They hurried on towards a magnificent building. As they approached they passed a frail and weak-looking young man who was praying. He appeared to be in a state of ecstasy and so Peter did not disturb him. Soon they reached the building.

'I did not wish to introduce you to that saint as he will be elsewhere as well,' said Saint Peter, mysteriously.

Who is he?' asked Shane.

'He is Saint Gerard Majella and many miracles are attributed to him.'

'How many saints are there?' asked Shane. 'I don't see many souls here.'

'They are very many, all of whom are working at God's tasks.'

They entered the building through a beautifully carved stone doorway and walked into a room of great size decorated with magnificent sculptures and paintings. The ends of the room were lost in the distance. The walls contained numerous rooms each of which had an entrance but no door. Shane stood and looked round him in amazement. He was overawed by the size and magnificence of the room and bowed his head in reverence.

'This is the Great Meeting Room for the hundreds of saints,' said Peter. 'It is capable of accommodating all the saints in heaven if necessary. A room is reserved for you here for prayer and reflection. In it you will find the Bible and other books such as Foxe's Book of Martyrs and an assortment of scrolls from the time of Jesus. Your room is along there on the right-hand side; you will find your name on the wall by the opening.'

Shane looked pleased. 'Wonderful,' he muttered.

Over some of the doors were inscriptions and Shane walked over and read the inscription over one door. It read as follows:

The will of God is done here, as God wills it and as long as he wills it.

Then looking around he saw a man levitating three feet above the ground. The man remained thus for a short time and then got to his feet. To Shane's surprise he was the same frail young man whom they had previously seen praying earnestly outside, a short distance from the building. He came over to the two saints and introduced himself.

'Welcome, Saint Peter, welcome, friend,' he said smiling. 'I am Saint Gerard.'

Peter introduced Shane, who asked the young man: 'we saw you outside some time ago. How did you get here before us?'

Saint Peter gently intervened. 'That miracle is a feature of Saint Gerard. He can be in two places at once. It is called bilocation. Gerard has performed many miracles. He is a Passion Level Two Saint and his patronage is for pregnant women.'

'Are you outside praying as well as being here?' asked Shane.

'Yes,' replied Gerard. 'I am. Other saints, too, can bilocate. It is quite usual. That is my room where you were reading the inscription.'

Saint Peter strolled out of the Saints' Great Meeting Room towards what looked like an ancient shop or a store. 'I'm satisfied with your responses to my questions,' he said. 'Heaven recognises your sainthood. Here,' he pointed to the old shop, 'is the place where your halo will be fitted.'

They entered and went to the counter where an elderly gentleman was serving. He had long, white hair and a thinning beard, both signs which indicated his extreme age. 'Joseph, my friend. How are you?'

'Well, thank you, Peter,' replied Joseph. 'Is that a new saint you have with you? I don't recognise him.'

'Yes. This is Saint Shane Grimshaw and he has passed the assessment to be given a halo. Shane this is Saint Joseph, the husband of Mary, the mother of Jesus. Joseph is a Compassion Level Three Saint as indeed is his wife. He is venerated by us all. He is the Patron Saint of workers and specializes in overseeing cabinetmakers and craftsmen on earth.' He turned to Joseph. 'Can you supply a halo for Shane, please?'

'I will have a look,' he replied. 'We have had a run on halos recently and my stocks are getting low. Please sit down, Saint Shane.'

Shane sat on a small dense cloud while Joseph measured the size of his head. Joseph took much care and tutted and muttered to himself as he worked.

'Can I have a square halo?' asked Shane.

The other two saints jumped. Had they had any breath they would have drawn it in sharply.

'Definitely not,' said Saint Peter. 'Square or triangular halos are only worn by the Holy Trinity. You may select the type of ring in terms of whether it is round or oval and its size, but nothing else. Goodness me – the very thought of it!'

Saint Joseph finished the measuring and then rummaged around in the almost empty transparent case of halos.

'Yes, I have one or two standard halos left. Now let me see. Which would be suitable for Saint Shane?' He muttered to himself while he took the halos out.

Much to Shane's disappointment the few in the case were not shining and looked dull and lifeless. Joseph eventually brought out four slightly different halos and presented them to Shane for his appreciation and selection. Shane hummed and hawed and made his choice.

'That one looks just right.'

'A good choice.' Joseph smiled at him. He placed it on Shane's head and they all admired the picture of holiness that Shane presented.

'It's rather like a small hat,' remarked Shane conversationally.

'Shall I switch it on now Peter?' asked Joseph.

'I think so,' replied Saint Peter.

Joseph turned back to his work surface and activated the halo, which immediately rose a little above Shane's head and emitted glorious rays of light. The others clapped their hands in delight.

'Glory be to God,' they said and prayed that Saint Shane would achieve all that his status promised.

'And a heavenly mobile as well, please, Joseph.'

Joseph turned again and rummaged in another transparent case full of new mobile phones. He selected one and handed it over. 'This is the latest model. Archangel Sariel has only just delivered these to me. You will be contacted on it when you are required for any purpose. It will also keep you informed of the latest news everywhere.'

'Supposing I lost it?' said Shane.

'These phones cannot be lost – they are homing phones. I have set it up on the new saint setting.'

Peter and Shane thanked Saint Joseph and they left his shop.

'We are nearly finished now,' said Peter. 'At least as far as I'm concerned, that is. There is much for you still to learn and all new saints are required to attend a Novice Saint's Course. This is run by the Third Choir Angels and your course will commence tomorrow. You will be a Level One Saint – Impassion. I suggest that you go to your room and pray for guidance. If you are humble, work hard at your patronage and pray as often as you can, you will advance your spiritual development and that of others.'

'Before you go will you answer me a question, please?' asked Shane.

'I must get back to my work at the Pearly Gates. Everything else you need to know will be discussed at your Novice Saints' Course tomorrow, but if it's a quick question then yes.'

'Will I be a Patron Saint and what will be my area of patronage?'

'I've been thinking about that,' replied Saint Peter. 'Patron Saints are those who have been allocated responsibilities for specific groups of people. If a mortal prays to you and asks for guidance your job is to intercede with God on his or her behalf. You will be informed how to do this on the Novice Saint's Course. Almost all saints have a group of people for whom they have a special area of responsibility. Joseph of Arimathea is the Patron Saint of undertakers, Magnus of Avignon is the Patron Saint of fishmongers, Giles is the Patron Saint of spur makers, though that is a declining area and I suspect that he will be allocated another area very soon. There are Patron Saints for lumberjacks (who are invariably an ungodly group), bookbinders, midwives, embroiderers, bricklayers (whose language leaves much to be desired), even politicians (whose behaviour leaves much to be desired) and many others; every area of mortals' activity is covered.

'There is one area where I think you will fit in very well. Currently there are two Patron Saints looking after that area, but it is an increasing area and there are more and more mortals praying to their Patron Saints for help and advice all the time. These are Saint Jude and Saint Gregory. I would like to put you with them. They, and you, will be the Patron Saints of Lost Causes.'

So saying Saint Peter left Saint Shane Grimshaw and walked back the way they had come.

7

THE MITIGATION OF GOD'S WRATH

In the beginning God created the heaven and the earth[15]. So much is clear. It is axiomatic that any management system set up by mankind should be monitored at regular intervals. Thus, the suitability and progress of any system can be assessed, and changes made to ensure its continuing effectiveness for its purpose. God made man in his own image[16] and thus it can be deduced that, if there is a system of monitoring on earth, it must be equally so in heaven. Logically, therefore, it should be expected that God regularly monitors his creations, both in heaven and on earth. He does.

'Could do better in spiritual areas and far too concerned with material gain. The commandments that God provided through Moses will, if implemented, be beneficial to all of mankind.'

---

15   Genesis 1:1.

16   Genesis 1:27.

God had recorded these comments in his little blue book about the earth.

Some two thousand years later God had thoroughly enjoyed the ludicrous antics of mankind, and the amount of entertainment that mortals had provided was well up to expectations. During this time, however, heaven had received only some short intermittent reports about the state of the earth and its inhabitants and certainly nothing like a full reappraisal, primarily because God's focus had been on other worlds. To rectify this omission, he decided to ask those angels who were responsible for monitoring earth's mortals, namely the angels and archangels, for an up-to-date assessment and a written report (in triplicate) of the situation. Thus, it came about that he phoned the Archangel Michael on his mobile.

'Good morning, Michael,' said God when he eventually got through. 'I hope you are well and that your wind problem is improving. I am aware that we have received no significant information about the planet earth recently and need an assessment and up-to-date report as soon as possible, please. A full report is required about all activities but with, of course, emphasis on spiritual matters and the implementation and acceptance of the Ten Commandments. I suggest that you consult Saint Peter who, as you know, is responsible for managing all immigrants from earth. He is currently either in the Saints' Village and Recreation Centre or at the Pearly Gates in Immigration. Just a moment and I'll find out.'

God then activated the tracking device on his mobile (Find a Saint) and soon located Saint Peter hard at work in Immigration dealing with the flood of new souls from earth. He spoke briefly to Peter, described the situation, and notified him of the urgency of the report. 'I'm sending Michael down right away,' he concluded.

Archangel Michael thanked God for the honour bestowed upon him and immediately acquiesced (he could, of course, hardly do otherwise). On reflection, he decided to take a couple of angels with him to act as scribes, and so he made his way to the Angels' Relaxation Room where most of them spent their spare time. There he found that four of his favourite angels were doing nothing more constructive than playing Monopoly. It was a celestial version of Monopoly in which the streets and buildings of earth had been replaced by streets and places with names with a religious connection. There was a Prayer Way, a Cassock Chase, Altar Square, The Angel Islington,[17] Communion Street and so on. The concept of money was incomprehensible to the angels and so they used blessings instead.

From the pile of blessings in front of him and the large number of churches and mosques on his part of the board (Cathedral Close), Archangel Uriel was clearly winning. He had just picked up two hundred blessings for passing

---

17   The Angel Islington was the only terrestrial property on the board the angels were using.

GO when Michael arrived and asked for volunteers for a special job. All the angels except Uriel volunteered immediately and declared the game null and void. Uriel also volunteered, but with perhaps less enthusiasm than Michael would have wished. He cashed in his winnings with an expression on his angelic face which said that he would have accumulated far more heavenly blessings had the game not been interrupted. He sighed and carefully placed all his gains in his blessings box and then they waited for Michael to explain why they were required. Michael quickly explained the situation and the group of five angels unfolded their white wings and flew all the way to the Pearly Gates.

There a rather harassed-looking Saint Peter was busy interviewing souls anxious to enter heaven. His halo had slipped to a jaunty angle. Normally Saint Peter dressed very carefully, and his untidiness was a sign that he was under some strain. A long line of the souls of men and women from all parts of the world stretched out before the tables. The mortals were all shapes, colours and sizes and impatiently jostled one another in excited expectation of acceptance. Much to their disappointment many were refused admittance (one or two bishops were livid) and these souls were asked to visit other rooms for implementation of the judgement against them. In some cases, and disappointingly all too often, they were escorted along a line of red arrows painted on the floor that led to a fire-blackened door. Each time the door was opened some steps leading down and down were visible. A wisp of smoke could be seen arising from the depths. Over the door was an inscription which rather frivolously read:

HERE IT IS – KEEP SMILING

In recent times it had been found necessary to widen the steps as so many souls were being asked to 'step this way, please.' A line of souls was silently and sadly making their way down the steps. A few, a very few, were smiling.

Putting aside his work for the moment, Saint Peter attended the angelic delegation and, after Archangel Michael had outlined his request, he decided that a discussion would be necessary in his private quarters near the Pearly Gates. Consequently, a cessation in the applicant's interviews occurred while the angels and Peter discussed God's requirements. It took far longer than anyone expected and grim were the angels' faces when the meeting finished. The scribes were hard pressed to keep up with the dictation and much paperwork was generated. Eventually it was finished, and the harassed Saint Peter returned to his work dealing with the queue of souls, which had grown by some thousands in his absence. His final words to the angelic delegation were: 'would you kindly ask God to allocate more resources to me, please. I'm getting close to the point of being unable to cope.' Promising faithfully not to forget, the angels made their way back to their conference centre.[18]

There they began to perfect their reports about which, it is sad to relate, they were not happy. The speed with which the scribes had worked had led to poor writing, which in some places was almost illegible. The re-writing had to be done somehow, however, and, as they feared that God would be displeased with their reports and, knowing that he was a stickler for accuracy and brevity, they took considerable pains in their composition and writing them neatly, in triplicate of course. At last they were satisfied that they could do no better and Michael sent a text message to God informing him of the availability of the reports.

God replied, also by text, asking: 'what reports are those?'

On being reminded that they were concerned with the earth, he replied: 'of course, that pesky little planet. Meet me in room eight in the Divine Conference Centre after evening prayers.'

They all gathered in the conference room as required and having preened and folded their wings, the nervous angels awaited God in silence. God arrived soon afterwards but, unfortunately, he was not in the best of tempers, having forgone a short nap while an angel would have played soothing music on a harp.

'Right,' he said, 'let's get on with it.'

---

18   Unfortunately, subsequent events were of so traumatic a nature that they completely forgot.

Archangel Michael took a deep breath and presented a summary of the reports the angels had prepared. 'I'm extremely sorry, my Lord, but the reports are not very encouraging.'

God quickly skimmed through the pages of the summary and as he read, his face grew blacker and blacker. The first part described the despoliation of the earth and how its resources had been squandered and used to build structures and systems of little use to the spiritual growth of mankind. Then it described the lifestyles of the peoples of earth: how they spent almost the whole of their lives in the pursuit of material gain, pleasure and matters of inconsequence. The final part was about mankind's non-conformance to the Ten Commandments and how endemic war and pestilence had resulted. As he read, the face of God grew blacker still. Eventually God finished reading the summary and sighed, and when he sighed, a rumble of thunder was heard throughout heaven.

He considered the matter for a moment. 'To summarize the conclusions,' he commanded, 'I will consider the Ten Commandments I gave to Moses and which he left as a guide for the mortal's development and wellbeing.

'Number One: *Thou shalt have no other Gods before me.* How did the mortals of earth deal with that commandment?'

'Very badly, Lord,' said Michael. 'In the past they have always worshipped many gods of their own devising and today they still do so, but above all they worship money,

money and more money. The second god they worship is pop music. These two gods come well above you in popularity.' He bit his tongue as he said the last sentence – it was not, perhaps, the most tactful way of putting it.

'I see.'

Lightning flashed around God's beard.

'Number Two: *Thou shalt not make unto thee any graven image.* How did they fare with that commandment?'

'Very badly, Lord,' replied Michael. 'Images of heaven and earth are commonplace. A few artists even make images of you. Idols are frequently worshipped and some mortals even regard THEMSELVES as superior to all others.'

'I see. I sense the hand of Lucifer in this.'

The lightning crackled angrily as it played around God's beard.

'Number Three: *Thou shalt not take the name of the Lord thy God in vain.* How did they manage with that commandment?'

'Very badly, Lord,' said Michael, sadly. 'Profanity, anger, malice, blasphemy and swearing are all commonplace, especially in broadcasting systems (whose influence on the populations of earth is highly significant). I didn't understand many of the words they used.'

'I see.'

Angry lightning crackled and flashed its way around the conference room.

'Number Four: *Remember the Sabbath day and keep it holy.* How did they fare with that commandment?'

'Very badly, Lord. On earth the Sabbath is a day just like any other. Much sport is played on the Sabbath. Excessive consumption of non-communion wine and other spirit-based liquids are also widely indulged in.'

'I see.'

The lightning became more intense.

'Number Five: *Honour thy father and mother.* I suppose that this commandment was ignored as much as the others?'

Michael was slightly happier to report the response to this commandment. 'No Lord, it was slightly better. Some of the mortals on earth do keep this commandment but unfortunately many ignore it.'

'I see.'

The lightning crackled with angry intense bolts.

'Number Six: *Thou shalt not kill.* I have deep reservations as to whether mortals were able to keep this commandment.'

This time Michael was trembling. 'You are right, Lord. Killing is widespread throughout the whole world. They kill for political reasons; they kill for monetary and material gain and they even kill for personal pleasure. Furthermore, killing is regarded as a legitimate form of broadcasted entertainments. They will kill anything that has lived, including themselves.'

'I see.'

The conference room echoed to the crash of thunder and blinding flashes of lightning as God's anger increased.

'Number Seven: *Thou shalt not commit adultery.* Did

they fare any better with this commandment?'

'No Lord. No notice is taken of this commandment by almost all mortals, from the lowest in status to the highest.'

'I see.'

The floor of the conference room vibrated and there was a deep rumbling as though an earthquake was imminent.

'Number Eight: *Thou shalt not steal.* How did they manage with that commandment?'

'Very badly, Lord,' said Michael. 'Stealing is endemic. Their houses of correction, of which there are many, are overflowing with miscreants, and represent a feeble attempt at social conversion. There is insufficient capacity to meet the demand for incarceration. I'm sorry to report that some of the biggest thieves are from their corporate structures and officials from every walk of life.'

'I see.'

A storm raged within the conference centre and Michael trembled.

'Number Nine: *Thou shalt not bear false witness against thy neighbour.* From what you have said previously, Michael, I hold out little hope of mortals keeping this commandment.'

'I regret to say that you are correct, my Lord. Here again, political and personal gains are paramount and far above any other consideration. The truth is rarely observed, and few believe this to be a sin.'

'I see.'

The lightning flashed, the thunder roared and as gale-force winds smote the conference room walls, the angels were compelled to fold their wings to protect themselves.

'Number ten: *Thou shalt not covet anything that belongs to another.* Tell me the worst about my final commandment.'

'The mortals again fared very badly, Lord,' said Michael. 'The cult of self above all is widely practised. For reasons of malice or simply improving their own status, the coveting of other people's property is endemic.'

The conference room was hit by raging storms. Lightning flashed continuously, thunder rent the atmosphere and howling winds tore at the room. Thunderbolts emanated from God as his wrath was vented. The angels huddled together to protect themselves from God's wrath. They trembled and dare not look upon the face of God. Instinctively they prayed for deliverance.

For a while God's anger was such that he could not speak. Eventually he calmed down and as he did so the storm raging in the conference room also died down. There was silence. Eventually God spoke softly: 'I created a world which should have become a paradise for mortals. Everything was provided to enable them to develop in relative peace and harmony but what did they do? They abused it. They destroyed it. My commandments are a social formula which supports a peaceful existence. They could have become prosperous in spiritual matters but instead what did they do? They disobeyed every one of my commandments; they did whatever they wanted regardless of the effect it had on others, but worst of all they have mocked ME – their creator and mentor. I despair of them ever becoming spiritual beings.'

He paused, and his brow furrowed with thought.

'I must consider how to deal with this miscreant race. I'm tempted to wipe the whole lot of them from the face of the earth. That would accord with my stated desire to impose vengeance on evil-doers.'

He paused and once again his brow furrowed in thought.

'I am, however, a merciful God, so annihilation may be too harsh a punishment; nevertheless, mankind must be punished. What form of punishment would be appropriate?'

The angels realised that the question was rhetorical, and that God was thinking aloud and so they said nothing. Eventually God thanked the angels for their help and stomped angrily back to his study where in the comfort of his favourite cloud armchair he considered what he would do.

With considerable relief at the termination of the distasteful interview, the shaken angels returned to their recreation room and attempted to continue with their game of Monopoly. Their concentration had been destroyed, however, and their play was abominable and so they soon gave it up, twiddled their thumbs and preened their wings.

God's thoughts about the future of mankind were varied. Initially thoughts of vengeance were uppermost in his mind and he seriously considered that wholesale destruction was appropriate. Then on reflection about how much work he had invested in the creation of the earth, and reluctant to waste it all, he thought about reducing the punishment to a few well-aimed thunderbolts and the eruption of every volcano. Then he contemplated raining down on earth a plague of hailstones, each one of which would weigh one talent, or creating another pandemic similar to the Black Death. He also considered exchanging the status of the very wealthy with the very poor and other similar ideas, but he soon realised that none of these ideas would have a positive effect on mankind. Nevertheless, he steadfastly refused to condone mortal activities but what should he do?'

Eventually he slept and during his sleep the solution came to him. He would give mortals one more chance before Armageddon was visited upon the earth. He had promised that his son would visit the earth for a second time[19] and whereas it had not been his intention for Jesus Christ to return in the foreseeable future, he could certainly bring it forward. On further consideration an alternative approach struck him. He ruminated and cogitated about it and the more he ruminated and cogitated the more it appealed to him. Eventually he found that the idea appealed to him so much that he started to chuckle.

---

19   Acts 1:11 and other references.

This turned into a raucous laugh and then a paroxysm of guffaws that continued until he was completely legless. With his good humour restored he decided to proceed and began putting everything in place.

Thus, it came to pass that in early December of that year a rumour became widespread throughout the earth that a visit by a celestial Messiah was imminent. At first nobody knew how the rumour had started: all the clergy from the different faiths all over the world denied being the originators of the rumour and no one else admitted responsibility. The communist party denied it, the scientists denied it and even the Flat Earth Society and The Women's Institute denied it. Nobody knew the date or the time, but believers in the Second Coming thought that as Christmas was approaching the visitation would be then. Soon after the first rumour circulated a second rumour appeared, the essence of which was to confirm the authenticity of the first. The leaders of the different faiths of the world then announced their belief in the authenticity of both rumours. This came about after they had all experienced a vision in which an angel had appeared announcing that a Messiah would indeed visit the world soon and once again advise mankind of its social and spiritual responsibilities. What had caused the initial denial by the leaders of the world's faiths was that none of them could believe that what they had been preaching about for thousands of years was really about to happen. The stated place for this celestial visitation was to be the Countess of Chester Hospital in

Cheshire, and the bizarre nature of this choice and its lack of "visible" holiness contributed to considerable and renewed disbelief. It was assumed that the Messiah would arrive in the same way that Jesus Christ had arrived – through a Virgin Birth, but nobody knew for certain.

Prophets then began appearing out of the woodwork (as it were) like magic. Couples claiming to be the potential parents of the holy child were common. Men from every country in the world claimed that their wives, or mistresses (or both), were pregnant with the holy child. There was one couple, however, a Sidney and Sharon Smith from Widnes, who for obvious reasons did not make that claim. They had been trying unsuccessfully for a child for many years and now that Sharon had reached the age of eighty-three, they had finally accepted that it wouldn't happen. One day in mid-December they were on their way to a pensioners' keep-fit evening class when Sharon was taken ill. An ambulance was summoned, and she was rushed to the Countess of Chester Hospital. There, much to the amazement of the doctors, she was declared to be in the final stages of pregnancy.

The news of Sharon's pregnancy soon became widespread and was reported in almost every newspaper and magazine in the country. The Daily Mail declared it to be a miracle – a declaration that was immediately refuted by the communist papers and the Ecclesiastical Times. Before the miracle could be accepted by the authorities some proof was required and the pregnancy was quickly confirmed by the gynaecological consultants at the hospital. Then, close to the time of the birth and to the amazement of all those present in the hospital, a number of strange phenomena occurred, suggestive that some celestial event of great importance was imminent. Huge numbers of shooting stars were seen over the hospital, cows and sheep started to gather in the fields around the ward where Sharon was located, and sounds reminiscent of a heavenly choir were heard. The Bishops of Chester and Liverpool felt compelled to attend to deny the common belief that the birth was a miracle and that a Messiah was to be born. Within a few hours, however, they were convinced of its authenticity and proudly announced to the world that the Second Coming was happening.

All these activities were broadcast to the nation on national television and drew the attention of the world to the Countess of Chester Hospital. Representatives of the world's media arrived in frantic urgency to ensure that they didn't miss the occasion with its inevitable huge advertising potential. Leaders of the world's religions arrived, and the hotel and bed-and-breakfast businesses did a roaring trade. It seemed that the whole world wanted to witness the birth of the child. The Archbishops of Canterbury, Westminster and York all agreed that the birth would be regarded as immaculate and as predicted in the scriptures.

The final evidence for a birth of celestial origin was seen when, two days later, the sky was lit by a heavenly, multicoloured glow that was more spectacular than any display seen on November 5th. The celestial host had arrived. A choir of angels was seen descending upon Chester. They hovered over the hospital singing the praises of the Lord and a second Virgin Birth. In the field next to the room where Sharon was confined, the bishops and archbishops elbowed the animals aside so that they could see better and fell upon their knees in prayer. Three elderly, bearded gentlemen arrived dressed in fancy clothes and proclaimed their status as Wise Men bearing gifts for the child and were highly indignant when a policeman was detailed to persuade them to move on to the nearest civic reception centre. The angelic choir sang heavenly music and the sky was filled with hordes of angels all singing and praying as it was announced that the birth was imminent. Then the birth occurred and to the amazement of everyone present, it was seen that the baby was a female. The Messiah was female. The Messiah was the daughter of an elderly couple from Widnes.

8

MESSAGES

Message scrawled on the south wall of Chester Cathedral:

The Kingdom of God is masculine. All imitations are false

Letter from the Right Reverend Montague Pound, the Bishop of Chester, to the Most Reverend Archibald Farthing, the Archbishop of Canterbury.
January 5th 2005

Your Grace,

It is my privilege and pleasure to respond to your letter requesting information about the child of Sidney and Sharon Smith. I'm sorry to say that the child is now an orphan as her parents both died a mere month after her birth. They survived long enough to have the baby baptised and this was carried out by myself in the cathedral on January 12th 2001. At her baptism she was given the name Eve.

You will recall the incidents surrounding Eve's birth when ecclesiastical opinion came to an understanding that Eve was the Messiah – the representative of God who was visiting the earth for the second time. The reasons for holding this opinion were as follows:

Firstly, rumours describing this 'Second Coming' had originated in every country in the world at the same time, thus indicating that it was highly unlikely that they had originated on earth.

Secondly, the age of Sharon Smith (eighty-three years old) was such that conception by the normal human means was impossible. Notwithstanding this miracle (and I understand that Mrs Smith's pregnancy and the birth of her child have now been ratified as a miracle), Mr Smith was physically and medically unable to have fathered a child. Clearly the conception can only have been miraculous. Furthermore, Mrs Smith was medically unable to sustain a pregnancy except by supernatural intervention.

Thirdly, during the final days of Mrs Smith's pregnancy, the heavens above the Countess of Chester Hospital, where Mrs Smith was confined, were subjected to numerous unexplained phenomena. It is clear that different observers experienced different phenomena, but all were agreed that visions were observed of heavenly manifestations included angels of varying rank who sang choral works of outstanding beauty. The subsequent display of an unparalleled son et lumière was also observed by many people including senior clerics, and televised to almost every country in the world.

You must be aware that many millions believe that this child is indeed the Messiah and that she represents the 'Second Coming' as foretold in the Bible. Immediately after the birth of Eve, the number of people attending Christian churches and undertaking baptism and confirmation reached unprecedented levels. I regret to report that this initial flourish of interest has not been sustained, and the number of baptisms has now fallen to previous levels.

The child is well and is normal and healthy. Her mother chose the name Eve as a reference and tribute to the first female. It is, I believe, a most suitable name. So far there have been no signs of her demonstrating any abnormal or supernatural powers, but it is still early days. Eve is usually a quiet and polite child who has accepted the loss of her parents with equanimity, which is not surprising as she must have little, if any, recollection of them. Her character and personality are still unformed, and we wait with interest to see how she develops.

She is being cared for under the auspices of a Reverend Mother from the Church of England – this being the faith of her parents – and her half-sister, Deborah.

I hope this is of interest to your Grace.

Yours in God – Montague.

&

Letter from the Right Reverend Montague Pound, the Bishop of Chester, to the Most Reverend Archibald Farthing, the Archbishop of Canterbury.
July 21st 2012

Your Grace,

It was with great pleasure that I received your recent missive concerning the progress of our child, Eve Smith. I am pleased to report that Eve is growing up quite naturally to be a competent and intelligent young woman.

Academically speaking she has attended school assiduously and although she is not the brightest child, she excels at subjects that are of particular interest to her. For example, her interest in mathematics is low and when asked why she mysteriously remarked: "there are other and better ways of doing things." Generally scientific subjects do not hold her interest, but she excels at languages and geography. Her religious studies can only be described as outstanding; her studies of the Bible are far advanced compared with her colleagues. It is almost as though she is already familiar with the stories in the Bible and their interpretation, and the instruction she receives serves only to refresh her memory. As far as non-academic studies are concerned, she is interested in music and is avidly learning to play the guitar.

On a personal note, she disdains many of the things that interest young women. She has no interest in fashion or her appearance and has resisted all attempts by her classmates to persuade her to wear lipstick and powder, or even to have her hair arranged according to the latest fashion. In this she has tolerated considerable teasing without any sign of rancour or annoyance. When teased she merely smiles and I'm sure this illustrates a remarkable sense of self-control in one so young. She is also a very determined young lady and once she has decided on a course of action nothing will dissuade her. Another aspect of her youth I find surprising is her interest in conjuring tricks and illusions. They have a remarkable fascination for her, and she will avidly watch any programmes about magic.

Eve is interested in many non-academic subjects and particularly those involving the welfare of others, which would be surprising in a normal child of that age. She is but twelve and yet has already expressed a desire to become a nun so that, as she says, "I will know more about how I can serve God." This is an admirable path for her to follow and one I would have expected in a Messiah. In fact, if she is indeed the person that popular opinion claims for her, I would certainly have expected her to follow this, or a similar, path.

Although she is friendly with everyone, she has her own circle of friends – perhaps I should call them admirers (it is too premature to call them apostles!) – and they appear to be very important to her.

She is a most interesting young lady and I would strongly advise you to meet with her. I feel that she would learn much from your Grace and that you in turn would learn much from her.

Yours in God – Montague.

❧

Letter from the Right Reverend Montague Pound, the Bishop of Chester, to the Most Reverend Archibald Farthing, the Archbishop of Canterbury.
August 15th 2012

Your Grace,

I am in receipt of your letter containing your opinions of our child, Eve, and thoroughly endorse your general approval of her. I agree with your assessment of her abilities and am convinced that whether she is, or is not, the Messiah, she is a child with a rare insight into Christian subjects. She is, as you observed, able to discourse about religious subjects with a confidence and conviction far in excess of a child of twelve and I can only conclude that that this knowledge has been absorbed through her current religious instruction. It is as if she has an eidetic memory and all information is stored in her memory as an image. Despite this feat of memory, her *understanding* of the concepts of our faith is extraordinary and cannot be attributed to a mere reproduction of learned facts.

The extent of her belief in God is also remarkable in one

so young, and the Reverend Mother has reported that she has often found Eve prostrate in silent supplication for prolonged periods before the altar in the Lady Chapel. The Reverend Mother has also reported that at certain moments in her private worship, Eve uses a language that is unrecognisable. I can only assume that this is a case of glossolalia. This is not a unique phenomenon, but it is certainly rare and particularly so in one so young. When questioned later Eve said that her worship was so intense that she was unaware she was praying out loud, let alone in an unknown language.

Her response to your questioning her about her future was also of interest. She had, as you are aware, previously told me that her intention was to become a nun, but her answers to you made it clear that although she will attend the courses attended by novices who wish to become nuns, the notion of this being her final objective in her life has been discarded or, at least, it would not form its main focus. Your suggestion that it could serve as an apprenticeship for some currently unspecified mission was most apt, but what this 'mission' could be is still unknown.

I am not entirely convinced that her abilities derive from some supernatural origin as there are many examples of precocious children exhibiting extraordinary skills far superior to adults. The child Mozart would be one such example, and Leonardo da Vinci was another gifted with unbelievable skills far superior to those usually observed in adults, let alone children. Even so, there is, as you remarked, a uniqueness to this child's knowledge that is almost overwhelming.

I fully understand your surprise at her question to you regarding your grand clothing. Her comment that Jesus Christ and his apostles did not wear such clothing on earth and, if you portend to be a senior adherent to Christian values, why do you, is, I am sorry to say, rather impertinent. Her additional comment about the Pope also wearing *inappropriate clothing* (my italics) can only be construed as the rudeness of juveniles. Of course, juveniles are often far too direct in their comments to respect others and I put this down to tactlessness rather than offensiveness. On her behalf I apologise to you and I hope you will forgive her.

Your suggestions for her future development are both pertinent and constructive and we will endeavour to carry them out diligently. I am pleased to report that Deborah, Mr and Mrs Smith's other daughter, and her husband are sensitive of their responsibilities in this matter.

Yours in God – Montague.

જી

Letter from the Right Reverend Montague Pound, the Bishop of Chester, to the Most Reverend Archibald Farthing, the Archbishop of Canterbury.
July 21st 2017

Your Grace,

I find it necessary to provide you with an up-to-date account of the progress of Eve Smith. She has served her term of instruction as a nun and successfully passed the stages of postulant and novitiate, and has taken her temporary and perpetual vows far earlier than other laywomen. She has greatly benefited from the experience and, I believe, her teachers have also benefited. She then undertook a period of contemplation and reflection in almost complete isolation which lasted for some months. The results of this were extremely surprising: she has decided that she wishes to communicate with the people in as many countries as possible, and her chosen way of achieving this is through the medium of pop music. She has declared that she will form a band with other nuns from Chester. I have previously mentioned that she learnt to play the guitar some years ago and her wish is to sing and play the guitar.

I was dumbfounded when she told me about this intention. It appears that there has been a complete change in her attitude towards her future and although one expects young people to change their minds as they mature, I was taken by surprise. It is almost as though she has received some form of advice or direction from some non-secular source, though I am unable to conceive what this source might be. Certainly, nobody in the cathedral would have advised such a move with the possible exception of the Dean who is more sympathetic to the views of the young and foolish. However, on my asking, he denied giving Eve any such advice.

This is not what I expected from a possible Messiah. Although my views on how a Messiah would preach during a 'Second Coming' are unformed (I try to keep an open mind about this), I assumed that some similarity to previous events would occur. I am compelled to say how disappointed I am. I had high expectations that Eve would make a major impact on Christianity in this and other countries and to discover that what she really wants to do is to sing and play the guitar is a shock greater than I can tolerate. Another disappointment is that her half-sister is fully supportive of her. I need to pray for understanding in this matter.

Eve gave the clergy in the cathedral a taste of the sort of music she wishes to play yesterday. She and four friends (girls who trained as nuns with Eve) all of whom were wearing their habits, set up their guitars and drums in a room and sang and played for one hour. The music was not to my taste, the solemnity and dignity of church music was completely absent, and we were treated to an hour of vulgar, raucous sounds which were quite out of place in a cathedral. I was unable to determine whether the music was adequate, but it seemed to me to be rather amateurish. To say that I found the music offensive would not be too strong an opinion. I noticed the Deacon wincing on a number of occasions and the Canon Precentor who is, as you know, almost completely deaf, was visibly disturbed.

Apparently, the group intend to call themselves 'The Nuns' and will be playing at gigs, I think that is the word, all over Cheshire in the immediate future.

My disappointment at this development is so great that I am compelled to review my belief that Eve is, in fact, the Messiah. I shall, as always, pray for guidance and understanding in this matter.

Yours in God – Montague.

❧

Graffiti scribbled on the wall of the house of an atheist:

God works in a mysterious way

❧

Article from 'Our Messiah Correspondent', in the *Daily Clarion*, dated May 23rd 2020 under the heading 'THE NUNS'.

A new all-female group called 'The Nuns' performed at a concert in the Manchester Arena last night to tumultuous approval. The five girls, all of whom are committed nuns and were educated in Chester, commenced their performance wearing their habits and veils. The curtain rose upon a single girl highlighted by a blue spotlight. This was their lead singer, Eve. The stage was silent until she began an unaccompanied hymn similar to a Gregorian chant. After three minutes a back curtain rose revealing three other nuns who joined in softly strumming guitars and one nun who beat out a gentle rhythm on the drums. These four accompanied their lead singer, whose chanting slowly changed into a tune of great beauty and feeling.

Eve then took up a guitar and gradually, through a judicious selection of tunes, all of which were original, the mood of the evening changed and became a fascinating mixture of exciting tunes and skilful guitar playing. The audience loved it and each song was vigorously applauded. Eve spoke to the audience before each song about the group and their work. She talked with confidence and with so much sensitivity that it was possible to feel a bond forming between her and the audience.

An intermission occurred after ninety minutes and then before the commencement of the second half of the programme, Eve talked to the audience alone for three minutes. For some unknown reason she spoke in a language which was quite unintelligible and yet some members of the audience appeared to understand what she was saying. Then the other four nuns re-joined the stage and played a striking chord on their guitars accompanied by a thunderous roll on the drums. This was immediately followed by them all discarding their habits and revealing raunchy and eye-catching clothing typical of female pop singers. This was a huge surprise to the audience who responded with cheering and whistling. Eve launched the second part of the concert with more songs and tunes of surprising originality, many consisting of sweeping arpeggios from the guitars interspersed with choral phrases from all five nuns. The audience loved it and went wild, shouting and whistling and demanding more. The Nuns' final tune was their own rendering of that old favourite: 'When the Saints go Marching in' and was delivered with panache and vigour to even louder and more sustained applause. The audience was not prepared to let the five nuns go and clapped and cheered until they had received what they regarded as their full quota.

This new group, The Nuns, is clearly destined to go far and we confidentially expect this music – popular music with religious and classical influences – to sweep the country. We have witnessed a completely new form of music.

❧

Graffiti on a wall in Manchester:

I swing with the nuns

❧

Letter from the Right Reverend Montague Pound, the Bishop of Chester, to the Most Reverend Archibald Farthing, the Archbishop of Canterbury.

May 23rd 2020

Your Grace,

I am amazed by the newspaper reports about the concert at Manchester Arena last night. It appears that Eve Smith and her colleagues have become remarkably famous almost overnight and I am deeply concerned about her welfare. I sincerely hope that this success does not have an adverse effect on her attitude towards life, but I fear it may well do so. She was brought up as a person with strong religious convictions which are in complete opposition to the life she is now embarking upon. Success, in terms of fame and its ensuing wealth, can have (I should perhaps have said invariably does have) an adverse effect on the character of the individual and I am full of concern that Eve and her companions have abandoned their spiritual life in favour of a materialistic one. Has she submitted to the attractions of a hedonistic life? Has Satan put such temptation in front of her that she is unable to resist? I am praying to God for help in understanding this development and would gladly value your advice.

Yours in God – Montague

P.S. I am distraught to find that my belief that Eve is the Messiah we had all hoped and prayed for has now been destroyed.

❧

Report in the *Bugle,* dated May 28th 2020 under the heading 'Wealth or Poverty.'

The newest singing sensation – the group called The Nuns – is in the process of becoming extremely wealthy. The revenue from their gig at the Manchester Arena on May 22nd has raised a sum in excess of two hundred thousand pounds and this paper questions how such wealth, with the prospect of a considerable increase in the near future, is consistent with a nun's vow of poverty that all nuns are required to take.

❧

Message scribbled on a wall of a charity shop in Chester:

Nunplussed – Confused of Chester

❧

Paragraph in the *Daily Clarion* from 'Our Messiah Correspondent', dated August 15th 2020 under the heading: 'Nuns release their Second Album.'

The singing sensations, The Nuns, have released their second album. This album is original music of the same quasi-religious nature as their first and is set to be equally as great a hit.

ಞ

Report in the music magazine *Trumpet* under the heading 'Nuns are Number One', dated November 25th 2020.

The latest album from The Nuns has remained at the top of the charts for the fifth successive week. The demand for their music has exceeded all estimates and forecasts. This group is well on the way to becoming a phenomenon and looks likely to overtake The Beatles and the Spice Girls in popularity.

ಞ

Graffiti on the north wall of the cathedral in Chester:

None but the Nuns

ಞ

Headlines and Report on the BBC Television Today Programme at 08.00, dated February 21st 2021.

MIRACLE AT WEMBLEY

Last night's performance by The Nuns at Wembley Stadium was as popular as ever. It was attended by ninety thousand people with more being prevented from entering the stadium, which has never been so full before. In terms of spectacle the programme content surpassed all previous engagements. The programme of quasi-religious and pop music accompanied by some remarkable visual effects was as phenomenally popular as before and wild scenes of approbation not seen since the days of The Beatles occurred on more than one occasion.

Almost halfway through the evening an incident of potentially staggering importance occurred. A handicapped teenage girl was injured when her wheelchair was upset during a moment of high excitement. She was thrown from her wheelchair and fell to the ground and was trampled on by the surrounding people. Nobody heard her screams for a moment and when it was realised what had happened paramedics immediately rushed to her aid.

The performing Nuns noticed that a disturbance was occurring in the stadium and stopped singing in the middle of a song. Eve, their main singer, then made her way over to the injured girl and helped the medical staff.

Our music correspondent reported that Eve spoke gently to the girl for five minutes after which the girl stood up and announced that she was completely better. She did not use her wheelchair again for the rest of the evening and was able to enjoy the remainder of the programme standing up without any discomfort or apparent injury. She was offered a comfortable seat by the stadium officials but declined the offer.

According to our correspondent, the medical staff said that they were unable to understand why after Eve Smith had spoken to her the girl's injuries were cured and why her permanent disability had apparently completely vanished.

We will bring you further details as soon as we have them.

❧

Headlines and Report on the BBC News at 13.00, dated February 21st 2021.

Earlier today we reported an incident at Wembley Stadium during a concert by The Nuns when a handicapped teenaged girl was injured and apparently cured by the lead singer of the group. The injured girl was Jennifer Brooks from London. Jennifer has suffered from polio since she was five years old. Apparently during an exciting part of the programme Jennifer's wheelchair was overturned, and her arm broken during her fall, or so the paramedics who attended her reported. After the lead singer from The Nuns came over and talked to her for a short time, Jennifer was apparently completely cured of all her injuries and disabilities.

We have since interviewed a consultant in the field of polio and another specialist in fractures and they are both adamant that a cure brought about through discussion is quite impossible. Both consultants have examined Jennifer and have confirmed that she is now showing no sign of polio and that her arm appears normal. Neither can account for the apparent healing that took place. Their conclusion is that the girl's arm was not fractured as first believed, and that her polio has gone into permanent remission. Both are convinced that no miraculous cure could possibly have been achieved.

The paramedics who examined Jennifer refute these comments and stand by their initial examination and conclusions.

Letter from the Right Reverend Montague Pound, the Bishop of Chester, to the Most Reverend Archibald Farthing, the Archbishop of Canterbury.
April 2nd 2023

Your Grace,

Again, I find that the activities of our child, Eve Smith, have caused me considerable unease. You are aware, of course, that the reports of the various cures of sick and injured people by Eve are being described as miraculous. I am unable to account for these phenomena, particularly as there appears to be no rational explanation for them and that various medical and religious experts are divided in the opinion as to what really happened. If I am to believe the reports, Eve has demonstrated the ability to cure people suffering from almost any ailment or disorder. Are these cures real and permanent? Are they miraculous? My heart tells me it is possible, but my head says otherwise. I recall with some disquiet that as a child Eve was fascinated by illusions and conjuring tricks and it is with considerable apprehension that I fear there may be a connection between the miracles and the illusions.

Eve and her friends' musical efforts have proved to be remarkably popular and have yielded enormous wealth. I find it impossible to believe that anyone with miraculous powers (if true, of course) could accumulate such wealth and yet still purport to be a committed nun and a child of Christ.

Furthermore, I am reliably informed that The Nuns' concerts have changed their presentation. Apparently as well as talking to the audience after each song, Eve now *preaches* to them before the last song. She talks about young people and the lives they live and how they can be improved. She does not mention the role of God in her preaching, but she is undoubtedly espousing Christian views to a section of the community who have ignored them for years. To my great surprise the audience are enthusiastically agreeing with her. I feel that she and her friends are influencing the attitude and lifestyle of young people in a positive way, a way that has previously proved to be impossible. As always, I would greatly value your comments and advice.

Yours in God – Montague.

❧

Two messages on a wall in South London:

God now lives with me in my house
That's funny because he's living in mine too

❧

Note from the Prime Minister, Sir Edward Longshanks, to the Home Secretary, Reginald Henry Thomas.
June 23rd 2023

Dear Reg,

I note your concerns about the influence that the popular singer, Eve Smith, is having on the lives of young people in the country. At present I do not share your concerns, but should her influence grow, as appears likely, then I think we could reconsider the matter.

Kind Regards – Ted.

❧

Paragraph in the Newspaper *Daily Reflection*, dated September 17th 2023.

It has been recorded that a new charity has been formed under the name SABBETH. Its objectives are to provide shelter for homeless people, food for those whose income is well below the average for the country, and advice on all aspects of living but with reference to the problems of the poor. It is unknown who is funding this venture as it is estimated that the costs are extraordinarily high.

The *Daily Reflection* believes that these objectives, which form part of the recent manifesto of the Social Democratic Party, should be immediately adopted by the Government.

❧

Note from the Prime Minister, Sir Edward Longshanks, to the Home Secretary, Reginald Henry Thomas.
March 23rd 2024

Dear Reg,

I have given considerable thought to your comments of last June and I believe that the time has come when we should seriously consider the matters relating to Eve Smith's activities. Her influence in our lives is becoming significant and we, ourselves, may be vulnerable to a rise in political interests which are in opposition to those of our own Republican Party.

I am proposing that we set up a committee to examine all facets of her life. It may be necessary to find some issues which can be used to manipulate the situation.

Kind Regards – Ted.

❧

Report in *The Trumpet*, dated May 11th 2024.

The new singing sensation, The Nuns, have now exceeded the popularity and wealth of all previous musicians. The attraction of their music has now spread from the young to the more elderly. Furthermore, their philosophy, which is based on Christian ethics, is also becoming equally popular.

❧

Letter from the Right Reverend Montague Pound, the Bishop of Chester, to the Most Reverend Archibald Farthing, the Archbishop of Canterbury.
July 2nd 2024

Your Grace,

I find the situation regarding Eve Smith more confusing than ever. There is no doubt that through her musical activities she has become popular beyond belief. As you know, I originally thought that she must be the Messiah who is promised will revisit the earth, but then her involvement in popular music appeared to disprove this. I also find that she and her colleagues have accumulated great wealth, which is completely opposed to our Benedictine ideas of poverty, and this was, for me, sufficient to reverse my belief in her celestial origin.

Now I understand that this charitable organisation SABBETH was set up by her managers *and at her instigation* and is entirely funded by contributions from her singing activities. I cannot but applaud such altruistic principles and it has endeared itself to me by its association with Christian values.

I find that once more my thoughts are clouded by doubts. Who is Eve Smith?

If we believe that the progress she is making in popularity and influence continues, I cannot imagine what the future will hold.

As always, your revered counsel on this matter will be much appreciated.

Yours in God – Montague.

Note from the Prime Minister, Sir Edward Longshanks, to the Home Secretary, Reginald Henry Thomas.
December 23rd 2024

Dear Reg,
The report from the committee considering the activities of Eve Smith will be issued to party members immediately after Christmas. It will be classified with the highest degree of security possible and is not, *under any circumstances*, to be copied by anyone. I have my copy which I shall send to you today and will be grateful for your private thoughts as soon as possible.

Kind Regards – Ted.

❧

Headlines and Report on the BBC News at 13.00, dated February 21st 2025.

Breaking News! It has just been announced from The Electoral Commission that a new political party has been formed. A management group, which included the singing sensations The Nuns, has registered its intentions to form a new political party to be called Benedictus. The new party will base its philosophy on justice and peace for all.

Further details will be released as soon as they become available.

❧

Note from the Prime Minister, Sir Edward Longshanks, to the Home Secretary, Reginald Henry Thomas.
February 28th 2025

Dear Reg,

Further to our discussions yesterday I have pondered long upon the necessity for acting in the matter of Eve Smith. I am aware that the fame of such artistes is often brief and that may be the case here. If that does indeed occur, then any action on our own part will be unnecessary. With the formation of this new political party, Benedictus, there is no doubt in my mind, however, that at present she represents a real threat to the stability of our current political processes and indeed to society itself, but that is currently unquantified. We shall be able to assess her influence far more accurately, of course, after the General Election next year.

Kind Regards – Ted

❧

Local Parliamentary Elections. Constituency of Chester. Returning Officer's Speech.

I, being the Returning Officer for the constituency of

Chester, do hereby announce that the votes cast in the General Election on May 20th 2026 were as follows:

Parsloe, Geraldine Mary.	Republican Party:	9,456
Grimshaw, Arthur Kingsley.	Social Democratic Party:	11,793
Smith, Eve.	Benedictus Party:	75,793
Eyes, Two Crossed.	The Silly Party:	568
Healey, Richard Aymes.	Independence Party:	1,034

I hereby declare that Eve Smith has been duly elected as Member of Parliament for this constituency.

Headlines and Report on the BBC News at 08.00, dated May 21st 2026.

HUGE GAINS BY THE BENEDICTUS PARTY.
Good morning. Here is the news. In the General Election the Benedictus Party has achieved huge gains over the whole country, including Scotland, Wales and Northern Ireland. Both the Republican Party and the Social Democratic Party have suffered huge losses; in many cases the candidates have lost their deposits. The Benedictus Party has achieved a staggering 246 candidates elected with an average swing of 74.7% and now forms the second largest party at Westminster. Never in a General Election has any new party achieved so many candidates at its first attempt. The

Republican Party has lost 128 seats but still just maintains an overall majority of 9 seats.

It is clear that the swing has come about through the votes of the young and those people in the lower income brackets, who appear to have voted almost unanimously for the Benedictus candidates; whereas the wealthier members of society have continued to vote for the older, more traditional parties.

The Prime Minister, Sir Edward Longshanks, was visibly shaken when the scale of the losses in his party was revealed. Our political correspondent in Westminster understands that the Social Democratic Party is equally shocked at the result and that consultations between the two previously major parties will take place as a matter of priority.

On hearing the result, the leader of the Benedictus Party, Eve Smith, said only that the will of God has been made apparent. When pressed as to what changes she would like to see in the governance of the country, she replied that God's intentions will be served.

આ

A highly confidential note from the Prime Minister, Sir Edward Longshanks, to the Leader of the Opposition, Mr Alfred Gore. Copied to the Home Secretary.
May 21st 2026. 22.00

Dear Alf,

It is clear to me and my colleagues that a shift in political thinking of seismic proportions has occurred in the country as a result of the General Election. You will appreciate, I am certain, that this represents a threat to the very existence of our conventional political parties and their policies which have successfully formed the basis of rule in our country for hundreds of years. This is unacceptable to any of our parties and I am prepared to act to restore the status quo. To do so, however, I need the support of all the traditional political parties and to this end I am proposing to hold a highly confidential meeting between the leaders of the relevant parties at Downing Street tomorrow morning at 10.00. I hope you will be able to attend.

Kind Regards - Ted

Headlines and Report on the BBC News at 08.00, dated May 25th 2026.

BENEDICTUS PARTY LEADER DISAPPEARS
Good morning. Here is the news. The disappearance of the leader of the Benedictus Party, Eve Smith, has been formerly announced by their deputy leader. She has not been seen by any member of her party or her friends

in the ecclesiastical community for three days and her whereabouts is completely unknown. Scotland Yard has been called in and issued a bulletin to the effect that insufficient time has elapsed since her disappearance to instigate a full search and investigation, and are confident that she has gone to a retreat for the purposes of contemplation and prayer.

A highly confidential note from the Home Secretary, Mr Reginald Henry Thomas, to the Prime Minister, Sir Edward Longshanks.
May 26th 2026

Dear Sir Edward,
The matter that was discussed on May 22nd has now been implemented and resolved.

Kind Regards – Reg

The BBC News for June 1st 2027 at 08.00.

In the Queens Honours List announced today, the Home Secretary, Reginald Henry Thomas, has been awarded a knighthood. Other honours are as follows…

❧

Graffiti scrawled on the walls of the Houses of Parliament.

God is great

❧

9.1
THE LADDER

PART ONE – THE CONTACT

It is a common and well-known phenomenon that elderly people have enormous difficulties with electronic equipment. Since electronic components are theoretically so efficient, they form a constituent part of almost every device and gadget that involves electricity. Hence for so many people life is fraught with equipment that has no instructions and occasionally behaves without logic or common sense. Computers are the worst offenders in this respect, and frequently and for no apparent reason suddenly decide to stop doing what they are asked to do and provide a cheeky message to the effect that:

You have performed an illegal operation

The operator has, of course, done nothing of the sort. He or she has performed an action which they have done hundreds of times before without any problem. Why should a computer suddenly behave like this? Nobody knows.

Modern telephones are equally as baffling and idiosyncratic and provide a whole range of bad behaviour and awkwardness. They have a plethora of buttons to press which purportedly provide a whole range of desirable benefits, but can I use them? Of course not. They steadfastly refuse to behave as they should.

So, one day when I received a surprising telephone call, I had no idea whether it was from a real person, a con merchant, or just an artefact of my telephone. The telephone rang with a short burst of: 'Jesu, Joy of Man's Desiring', the famous tune from J.S. Bach's cantata. My telephone is equipped with different ringtones so that I can easily identify the type of caller: friends, family, ex-colleagues, etc. Bach's cantata was not one of the ring tones I had selected for any person or group of persons I knew, and I had no idea who it was who wanted to talk to me. Setting aside my apprehensions I answered the phone.

'Hello,' I said. I never give my name to unknown persons on the phone.

'Good morning,' said a very well-spoken voice. 'My name is Sariel and I'm calling you from heaven.'

Heaven? Clearly, this was a madman, a con merchant or a joker who had decided to call me.

'Yes, yes,' I replied in a voice heavy with sarcasm, 'and I'm the Archbishop of Canterbury. Thank you very much but I have all the blessings I need for today.'

I felt rather satisfied that I had managed to make an appropriate reply on the spur of the moment and ended the call.

A moment later I heard the cantata coming from my phone again. Clearly the joker was an obstinate man. Occasionally I received calls like this and when they were persistent, they were a real nuisance. It then occurred to me that this was a unique call and I could have some fun with this person, so why shouldn't I go along with him? It would provide me with a few moments of comic relief and I might even be able to put him off, so I answered the phone again.

'Mr Baptiste?' asked the softly spoken voice again. 'I'm really sorry for interrupting your day but I would be very grateful for a moment or two of your time.'

'OK,' I said. 'What was your name again?'

'Thank you so much. My name is Sariel.'

'Sariel? That sounds like a familiar name. Now where have I heard that name before?'

'My full name is Archangel Sariel,' replied the voice. 'There are many angels in heaven, as you are aware and I'm sure you will have heard of some of my companions: Michael, Gabriel, Raphael and Uriel. They are just some of the angels who are well-known on earth.'

Clearly, I was talking to a very disturbed person. It was, after all, utterly inconceivable that a telephone link existed between earth and heaven. Heaven had no need for such a line of communication; there were other and more effective methods of communicating with people on earth. It was a preposterous idea. Nevertheless, the telephone call was proving to be quite interesting and so I decided to humour the caller.

'If we are to have a meaningful conversation I have to call you something,' I said. 'Would you prefer me to call you Archangel Sariel or Your Angelship or what?'

'Just Sariel or Mr Sariel will do nicely,' replied the voice.

'Do you have wings?' I asked curiously.'

'Certainly. All angels have wings that are rather large and can be a little cumbersome at times, but they really are the best way of getting around heaven.'

'But I understood that there was no atmosphere in heaven. On earth we humans breathe air which, as you must know, is made up mainly of nitrogen and oxygen. Without air we humans would all perish.' (I liked the word "perish" as it had a sort of biblical feel about it. I thought it would be more appropriate than the word "die".) 'Furthermore, the air serves other purposes as well. Without an atmosphere flying would be impossible. As there cannot be any air in heaven I don't see how you can possibly fly.'

'Yes,' replied the self-styled angel. 'You are quite right *for earth*. Heaven is different. All the paintings that humans have made about heaven (some of which are very fine, I must say) show that there is gravity in heaven. Your conception of what goes on in heaven is quite erroneous. There is neither atmosphere nor gravity for the simple reason that we have no need for them. If there were any such needs, then God would have provided them.'

Smart-arse, I thought to myself. However, I believed it would be imprudent to say that to the madman on the end of my telephone. Instead, I said to him: 'what puzzles me is how you can use my telephone at all. I didn't know that BT had a line which could be used to contact heaven.'

'Ah. There is a lot about heaven and its occupants that the people on earth know nothing about. As it happens, electronics are my speciality and I devised the line myself.'

I chuckled at that. It sounded like another load of nonsense.

'All right, Mr Sariel,' I said. 'What is it that you wanted to ask me about?'

'Thank you, Mr Baptiste. You are too kind. I am only making a delivery. By the authority of heaven, I'm authorised to give you a message and to offer you a job.'

'A message? A job? I thought that messages from heaven came in the form of disembodied voices speaking to men and women when they are asleep.'

'Yes, that is certainly one method of communication we use with mortals. It was the preferred way we spoke to you two thousand years ago. I feel though that in this present era that method would lack credibility. For example, if I spoke to you when you were asleep what are the chances that you would believe me sufficiently to act on my words? Slim, I think. However, by speaking to you over the telephone you know that I'm a real person.'

'Well, yes,' I conceded, 'that is certainly true, but to be perfectly honest, Mr Sariel, although I've no doubts that you are a real person, I have considerable doubts as to your being an angel from heaven who is going to offer me a job. Consequently, I feel there is little point in continuing this conversation – as interesting and pleasant as it has been.'

'Oh, but there is, Mr Baptiste. I quite understand your difficulty in accepting my occupation and purpose. I anticipated that you would entertain such doubts, so I have a suggestion to make which will, I'm sure, help overcome them.'

Although the man was persistent, he was most polite, and I didn't really feel like terminating the conversation at that moment as I was enjoying it immensely. I wondered, too, what the message could possibly be that he wanted to pass on.'

'I propose,' continued the angel from heaven, 'that I ring off. Then I shall send you a message in your sleep. After that, if you will be so kind, please consider who I am and the next time we speak ask me any questions you wish which would help you to believe that I am genuine. When you are satisfied with my answers and your doubts have been allayed, I shall give you the message. Is that satisfactory? I suggest that you phone me at any time you wish, day or night, using the following number:

	PRESS 4 TWICE
then	PRESS 3 TWICE
then	PRESS 2 ONCE
then	PRESS 8 THRICE
then	PRESS 3 TWICE
then	PRESS 6 TWICE

'Ask for Help Desk Four and then for Archangel Sariel. I shall always be available. I must emphasise that the message is vitally important for you and for mankind. Thank you very much for your kind attention. I hope you have a good day.'

'How much will this call cost me?' I asked before he had time to ring off. A telephone call to heaven must be very expensive (unless it was on a free tariff) and I certainly didn't want to incur vast telephone bills.

'Nothing,' replied Sariel shortly, 'and I'm disappointed that you asked that question.'

The telephone went dead, and I put the receiver down feeling utterly confused. What on earth was I to make of all that? The man was obviously suffering from a very strange delusion and my common sense told me to forget all about him and his message. I imagined that he must be some kind of salesman; wasn't that one reason why strangers invariably cold-called other people. Then I remembered that I had increased the security settings on the phone recently and all messages, apart from those from people on my approved list, were blocked. Was he a salesman who had somehow managed to get past my security settings? It seemed unlikely. But if he was, and had, what could he be selling? He hadn't mentioned any product or even hinted at anything. Was he a practical joker? Then another thought struck me. Surely, surely, he couldn't possibly be the person he claimed to be? No, no, I just couldn't bring myself to believe that. Neither archangels nor angels spoke to people on the telephone. These beings only communicated to humans in biblical times; there had never been, as far as I could recall, any incidents of such telephone conversations being held in modern times. Then I remembered that telephones had only been invented in 1876, so telephone conversations from before that date were impossible. This might perhaps be the first such contact, but my common sense said it couldn't possibly be.

My mind refused to believe the caller was genuine, and I soon forgot about the matter. At least I did until I went to bed that night. As I climbed into bed the thought occurred to me that that I might just receive a message during my sleep. Once again, my common sense told me it was impossible, but even so I left a piece of paper and a pencil on my bedside table while deriding myself for being such a fool. It was not surprising, therefore, that I couldn't get to sleep.

I tossed and turned for a couple of hours but then, of course, I did eventually manage to sleep and for the remainder of the night I slept very well. It was quite dreamless, and I awoke with not the slightest remembrance of any voices and the paper by my bed remained unsullied by any hasty scribble. Well, I thought, that confirms that; I have been well and truly hoaxed, and for the rest of the day I forgot all about my telephone conversation with an angel from heaven. In the evening I went out to the pub with some friends of mine and told them about it and we all had a good laugh.

'A different sort of experience,' said Tom. 'I wonder who it was? Was it you, Dick?'

'It's funny you should say that,' he replied.

'If it was genuine you could have asked who the winner of the Grand National was going to be,' said Harry. 'That would be certain proof.'

Such was the attitude of my friends and I decided there and then that I would not mention the matter again; I could see that ridicule awaited me if I talked about it seriously.

The following night I went to bed as usual and because there was nothing on my mind I fell asleep almost immediately. To my surprise (or at least my surprise when I later recalled the incident) the dreams started at once. I often dreamed and was familiar with their apparently bizarre and vivid nature, and I've never ceased to be surprised at the impermanence of dreams. At some time during that night, I became aware of a voice talking to me.

'Mr Baptiste,' it said. 'Mr Baptiste. Listen to me, watch and remember.'

Even while the dream was in progress I can recall being astounded that the voice was the voice of my caller from heaven. It was the same soft and gentle voice, but this time I detected a sense of authority. It repeated my name for some time as though it was determined to get my almost completely unconscious attention. Then a dream started and I saw a ladder set upon the earth. It stretched as far as heaven itself, and on this ladder the angels of God were ascending and descending. There was a man standing at the foot of the ladder and to him a voice from above said something about the land on which he stood being given to him and his descendants. Then suddenly I was at the foot of the ladder. I woke immediately and when I had recovered sufficient consciousness I wrote down all that I could remember. The voice had said more about dust and seed but the memory of this part of my dream was so transient that I was unable to write it all down before I had forgotten it.

The following morning I rose and read my notes. Was there some significance in it all or was it just a figment of a dream caused by some mental aberration? I was reminded of my weird telephone conversation two days before. Was it the angel Sariel who had spoken to me? What was the significance of the ladder? Who was the man at its base and what was he doing? I had never heard or read anything about a ladder in these circumstances before. If it was indeed a message from Sariel then why didn't he make his meaning clearer?

I puzzled over it for a long time and eventually it occurred to me to see whether there was any reference to this dream in the Bible. It took me a long time and I had almost given up, but eventually I did find it. It was in the Old Testament in Genesis: chapter 28, verses 12 to 14 and it was a passage that I had never heard about before. The man at the foot of the ladder was Jacob. With mounting excitement, I realised that there was no doubt that this account was identical to my dream, but what did it mean and what was it to do with Sariel? Was it all nothing but a strange coincidence? On reflection I felt that somewhere there had to be a connection with the angel.

Having made a small amount of progress I decided to find out all I could about the angel Sariel. I looked up the references to him on the internet and found that there wasn't much at all, and the little I found was typical of characters in the Old Testament. It seems that Sariel was one of seven angels who were credited with primordial powers (whatever that meant). He was an angel of death, having obtained this reputation when he brought Moses' soul into heaven. He also brought Enoch's soul into heaven and some reports said that he was associated with the moon and its movements. That was about all I found and it all seemed to me to be rather unconnected and bizarre. Not much help there. I could see nothing to associate Sariel with Jacob's ladder and was about to disregard the information when I came across a footnote which said that it was *Sariel who had explained the significance of the ladder to Jacob.*

I was thunderstruck. Exactly as my telephone caller had promised I had received a message from him in the old biblical way of contacting humans. The significance of the ladder (which concerned the ethnic origins of God's chosen people) was irrelevant to me – I was merely interested in its apparently proven connection with Sariel. I thought about all this for a long time and found that I was eventually tempted to give some credence to the man purporting to be the Archangel Sariel. My reason disputed this, but my heart seemed to want to believe it. Temptation is a terrible thing and I found that the temptation to phone that strange number he had given me grew and grew until at last my curiosity overcame my doubts and I decided to call him.

The best time to call him, I decided, would be the evening, mainly because at that time calls to places abroad (and surely heaven was abroad) would be cheapest. Even though Sariel had said that calls to heaven would be free I still didn't have complete conviction that this would be the case. Taking my paper with the number I had scribbled down from the drawer by my bed I studied what I had written. It said that to call Sariel I should ring as follows:

	PRESS 4 TWICE
then	PRESS 3 TWICE
then	PRESS 2 ONCE
then	PRESS 8 THRICE
then	PRESS 3 TWICE
then	PRESS 6 TWICE

The first thing that struck me was that there was no area code. Surely an area   code for a department in heaven would be necessary? I thought that 01 would have been the preferred choice but other places had already appropriated that code and it would be rather confusing if one rang heaven instead of major city! The second thing was the bizarre nature of the dialling options. Press 4 twice, then 3 twice etc. Wasn't that a waste of dialling options? Why not something simpler? Anyway, if I was going to proceed with this nonsense I would have to obey the rules. Then to my surprise I found that I was trembling a little. The thought of really phoning heaven was slightly daunting, to say the least. A large glass of wine helped settle my nerves and I took the plunge and dialled the number as directed.

Much to my surprise I heard a tone as clearly as a bell without a hint of any crackle of interference. There was another surprise when someone answered.

'Hello,' said a female voice. 'Help Desk Four. Atarah speaking. How can I help?'

'Er, hello,' I replied felling extremely foolish. 'I would like to speak to Help Desk Four please.'

'Yes, sir,' replied the voice. 'This is Help Desk Four. Would you be so kind as to give me your name and tell me whom it is you wish to speak to.'

My confidence was growing all the time. 'My name is Jean Baptiste. My name is French because my parents were both French, but I was born in England.' I don't know why I proffered this unasked-for information but perhaps it was nerves.

'Thank you, Mr Baptiste. With whom do you wish to speak?'

I was highly embarrassed at having to say what I had to, but taking a deep breath the words stumbled out.

'I w-wish to s-speak to Sariel, that is A-Archangel Sariel.'

This, too, was accepted without comment.

'Just a minute while I put you through.'

There was a pause of a few seconds before a familiar voice came on the line.

'Mr Baptiste?'

'Yes, I'm here.'

'Thank you for calling. Have you satisfied yourself that I am indeed the Archangel Sariel?'

'Almost, but my total conviction rests upon you informing me what message you sent me and how it was delivered.'

'I sent you a message about Jacob and his ladder in the form of a dream which I hope you received.'

'I certainly did but it took me a long time before I found the connection between you and that incident described in Genesis.'

'There was a good reason for that,' replied Sariel. 'I needed you to have the faith that the message was from me and to do that you had to find the connection yourself.'

I was still amazed by all that was happening to me. The evidence that it really was Archangel Sariel who had phoned me on my landline was beginning to mount up. Now instead of doubting the evidence of my eyes and ears

I was trying to find reasons why my caller could *not* be an angel and that was proving to be more and more difficult.

'Can you describe what happens in heaven?' I asked.

'In heaven we worship and praise God – the creator of all things – and we try to emulate him in all matters. We work to serve the Lord here and for the betterment of *all* others on earth and all the other planetary systems that God created. Does that help you?' replied Sariel.

'Er, yes. Are there people from religions apart from Christianity in heaven?'

'Of course. The Bible makes that quite clear. It is one of Jesus' sayings and is recorded in the Gospel according to Saint John: chapter 14, verse 2. I quote:

In my Father's house are many mansions: if it were not so I would have told you.

'This means that for everyone whose life conforms to the precepts of Christianity and God's Ten Commandments will find a place in heaven. Status, wealth, fame and so on count for nothing in heaven. It is *how* you behave not who you are that matters.'

I was again overwhelmed by these answers. They contained no hint of secular matters – just the opposite, in fact. At last, I found I believed wholeheartedly that my telephone caller was the angel he claimed to be. I could see no alternative.

'Thank you,' I said. 'From the information you have

provided I believe that you are indeed who you claim to be.'

'Good. Then we can proceed to the message I have been entrusted to deliver to you.'

I waited with considerable trepidation. What on earth could a message from heaven to me, of all people, possibly be about?

'Mr Baptiste. I am sorry to be the bearer of bad tidings. I will quote from the Bible again. This time it is from the Second Epistle of Saint Peter: chapter 3: verse 10.

But the day of the Lord will come as a thief in the night; in which the heavens shall pass away with a great noise, and the elements shall melt with fervent heat, the earth also and the works therein shall be burned up.

'God has determined that the time is not yet right for the heavens to pass away, but that the end of the world is approaching and I am authorised to warn you of this fact.'

9.2

THE LADDER

PART TWO – THE PROPHET

'The e-end of the world? Are you sure?' I stammered.

'There is no doubt,' replied Archangel Sariel, dryly. 'This information comes from the highest authority.'

My mind reeled at this statement and when I had eventually accepted it, common sense prevailed.

'But on many, many occasions in the past the end of the world has been forecast and not once have any of these forecasts been correct.'

'You are quite right, but you must remember that all those forecasts were made by mankind, not God. This time the forecast is not a forecast but a certainty. We have been informed by God that it will happen.'

'Why?' I asked.

'Because mankind has refused to obey the precepts and commandments that God demanded. On two occasions God has sent his representative down to earth to advise and help mankind, and on each occasion the advice has been almost completely ignored and his representatives disposed of. The first, Jesus Christ, was, as you know, crucified, and the second, Eve Smith, as you may not be aware, was permanently incarcerated in some secret government asylum. God's patience is not inexhaustible. "Vengeance is mine," sayeth the Lord. Do you not recall that God's statement is recorded in different places in the Bible?'[20]

'Good Lord!'

'Yes, indeed,' said the angel enthusiastically.

'When will it happen?' was all I could ask.

'Within the next six months.'

He paused as if to let the importance of his words sink in.

'I appreciate that this must be a surprise to you. Consequently, I suggest that you ring off and when your mind has assimilated the information, ring me once more and we can discuss the task I have for you.'

I felt weak and feeble. My mind was still grappling with the enormity of the concept of the world's destruction.

'Right,' I muttered. 'I shall phone you again soon.'

The next few days were traumatic to say the least. Once more doubts as to the authenticity of my caller began to creep into my mind. It had taken me considerable mental agility to believe that I really had been having a discussion with an angel, but now he (or should that be it?) wanted

---

20   Romans 12:19 and other references.

me to believe that the world was doomed. I sat in my armchair looking out at my garden. In the distance I could see trees, fields, hedges and all the beauty of the English countryside in early summer. On the horizon I could see the distant buildings of Chester. Was all this about to be destroyed? How could I really believe that?

Then I recalled that strange affair when it was claimed the Messiah had been born in the Countess of Chester Hospital about thirty years ago. Despite the initial doubts of the ecclesiastical community, a baby girl had been born to an elderly barren couple and it was initially claimed that the child was indeed the promised Messiah; the Second Coming, as forecast in the Bible, had occurred at long last. This had initially led to a huge interest in biblical matters and churches were again as full as they had been in the old days. Within a couple of years, however, much of the world's population had reverted to secularism, a state that was quickly followed by hedonism. This was essentially due to the British Government's position denying the authenticity of the Messiah who, bizarrely, had disappeared shortly afterwards and was never seen again. The return of the peoples' interest in materialism was rapid and, although there were still a few adherents to the Christian faith, within a short time it was as if the purported Messiah had never existed. I had come to believe that the Messiah had indeed returned to earth and if I accepted that why couldn't I accept that the end of the world was imminent? Eventually I concluded that I had no other option than to phone the angel again and find out what tasks I was going to be required to carry out.

Two days later I phoned that strange number again and asked to be put through to Help Desk Four. Once more the line was crystal clear and a credit to whoever had devised the line – presumably Sariel himself.

'Hello, Mr Baptiste.' The same by now familiar quiet voice of Sariel answered me. 'Have you considered the message I gave you?'

'Good morning,' I said politely. Just because the world was ending there was no reason not to be polite. 'Yes, indeed and I'm prepared to carry out whatever task you set me.'

'Excellent. I always believed you would cooperate. I should point out, however, that there is no morning, afternoon, evening or night here in heaven. Your greeting of good morning has no meaning here.'

'Sorry, I wasn't thinking straight.'

'It is of little import. Now then, the task that God has set you. He has resolved to warn the people of earth that their total demise is imminent. He wants to give them   time to repent of their sins. You have been chosen to be the instrument of this warning for the people of Great Britain. You are the chosen one. You will be the prophet of God.'

'Me? Why on earth me – a bachelor with no ties?'

'Think of your name – Jean Baptiste. Two of your millennia ago there was another man with the same name as yours. The Gospel according to Saint Mark states that John the Baptist's task was to fulfil a prophecy from the Book of Isaiah which proclaimed the coming of the Messiah. You will fulfil a similar task and proclaim the end of the world. You are the perfect choice. I should add that a similar task is being given to one carefully selected member from each of the countries of the world.'

'But I have no experience of public speaking and my words will make me a figure of ridicule.'

'Do you not trust in the Lord? He will put the words of your proclamation into your mouth. He will raise you up and you and your fellow prophets will be exalted above all others. Most of the peoples of earth will perish in the forthcoming Apocalypse. Few will be saved. You will be saved if you have carried out God's task.'

'You want me to pronounce that the end of the world is imminent. Would it not be kinder for the human race not to know that its world is being destroyed by the very God that they have worshipped?' I asked.

'Mankind has had its chance. It has chosen hedonism over spiritual joy,' replied the angel. 'God has spoken, and it is not for me to question his demands.'

I thought about this. 'On reflection, if the world is to be destroyed within six months, I can think of no better way of spending my last few days than doing as you ask.'

'Doing as God asks – not me. I am only the messenger.'

'Can you tell me how the world is to be destroyed?' I asked.

'That I don't know,' replied the angel. 'Perhaps it is better that the people of earth are left in ignorance of that point.'

'You may well be right. Sometimes it is better not to know the precise form that the future takes. I will do as you ask.'

'Excellent. I wish you all good fortune.'

Those were the last words I heard from Archangel Sariel.

I paced the room as I considered all that we had discussed. How could I carry out my task when I had no experience of public speaking? As a humble and very junior clerk in a factory that made pork pies, I had never been required to make speeches. I didn't even know whether I could speak in front of a group of people. It was necessary for me to plan a course of action.

I considered what to do and on reflection it was clear that for me to walk about the streets of Chester wearing an advertising board proclaiming that the destruction of the world was upon us would serve no useful purpose at all. I would be mocked, ridiculed and perhaps pitied but NOT taken seriously. How could I get my message across to a wider population and preferably a responsible one? I pondered and cogitated and then wished that God would help me. After all, Sariel had promised that God would find the words for me so why shouldn't he help me plan my course of action? Then, as if in answer to my wish, it came to me. I would use my telephone discussions with the angel as a way of obtaining national publicity.

I would write to the newspapers and the broadcasting

organisations and hope that at least one would grant me an interview.

I sat down and, accompanied by feelings of apprehension at the thought of considerable verbal and possibly even physical abuse, started to write letters. To my surprise the words came quite easily and as soon as they were finished, I posted the letters in the knowledge that there was no going back. I was committed.

That evening I sat and reflected upon my strange task and how I would cope during the next few months. How would the end of the world come about? Would a fusillade of lightning bolts strike every country? Would the machinations of worldwide politics lead to the unleashing of a nuclear war? Would some worldwide plague affect every continent? Then another thought occurred to me. I suddenly realised that unless humanity knew *why* the world was being destroyed the whole event would be pointless. We might not know *how* the Apocalypse would happen until it did, of course, but we would be told in advance *why* – by me and my fellow prophets in all the other countries. Having reached this comforting speculation as to the importance of the purpose of my task, I went to bed early.

The next day the telephone rang first thing. It was the BBC.

'Mr Baptiste?' asked a voice. Then when I admitted the fact, it went on: 'we would like to interview you about your remarkable allegations. Could you get to our Manchester studios by midday today?'

'Certainly,' I agreed.

A moment later the phone rang again. It was the *Daily Clarion* making a similar request. Then six other newspapers called, followed by ITV. I did what I could to satisfy these organisations and then left to catch the train to Manchester. It was a very hot day, much hotter than was usual for that time of the year, and when I arrived at the studio I was delighted to find that it was air-conditioned and wonderfully cool. I was met at the television centre reception and immediately taken to a recording room. After just a short wait a senior interviewer from the news department came in. This was John Longworth, a man who in his interviewing techniques was as ferocious as an attacking Rottweiler and was universally feared. Had I known that it would be he who would be interviewing me then I might well have declined the invitation. My heart sank, and I confess that it was thumping away in my chest. I knew that I was in for a hard time and wondered whether I could handle it.

Longworth started the interview by introducing me and describing the alleged (as he put it) telephone conversation I admitted to with the Archangel Sariel as I had outlined in my letter.

'Can you confirm that my account of your experience is correct, please, Mr Baptiste?' he asked.

What he had said was inaccurate. The words in my letter had been deliberately misinterpreted and I said so, and without allowing him to interrupt me, I described exactly what had happened. I could see the look of total disbelief on his face and so I asked him: 'tell me Mr Longworth. Why did you distort what I had written in my letter?'

'Did I distort anything? I think not, but I made some logical inferences and deductions. That's all.'

'Those inferences and deductions were completely wrong,' I said.

'I think not. Have you ever had any mental problems or been admitted to any institution for the mentally disturbed, Mr Baptiste?' he continued.

'No,' I replied. 'Have you?'

'Certainly not, but then I don't make claims that I've been talking to angels.'

'Do you think that Moses or Jacob or any other of the hundreds of people who spoke to God in biblical times were deranged as well?'

Longworth smiled. 'The evidence for those claims is unconvincing. There is nothing but word of mouth to support them.'

'Do you not then believe anything you read in the Bible, Mr Longworth?' I asked.

'We are concerned with your beliefs, not mine,' he replied. 'You must agree that for someone to claim that he has been talking to an angel is to invite suggestions of derangement.'

'I dispute that.'

'Why?'

'Uniqueness does not infer mental derangement. Quite the contrary, in fact.'

'Have you ever met anyone called Sariel before?
'Never.'

'Did you have any difficulty in believing that your caller was an angel?'

'Certainly. At first, I did not, and could not, believe he was who he said he was.'

'What convinced you that he was an angel then?'

'He understood my difficulty in believing he was genuine and promised to provide me with proof. He said that he would send me a message.'

'What form did this message take?'

'He didn't say but two days later I had a dream about a man standing at the foot of a ladder which reached from earth to heaven. Then a voice spoke to the man. I felt sure that it was God speaking to him. I woke up and wrote down all that I could remember in my dream.'

'So how did that prove it was an angel who had spoken to you on the phone?'

'I did not understand why either, so I looked for a description of my dream in the Bible. There I eventually found it recorded exactly as I had dreamed. I also learnt that the man at the foot of the ladder was Jacob. According to the Bible Jacob did not understand the reason for the ladder but I later discovered that it was the Archangel Sariel who explained the significance of the ladder to him.'

'So, you took that as proof of the authenticity of your telephone caller?'

'I did.'

'I don't find that in the least convincing.'

'You don't surprise me. The whole of your interviewing technique is based upon disbelief and doubt, the reason for which is obvious: you are trying, unsuccessfully I might add, to prove that I am a charlatan and a fraud.'

'I put it to you, Mr Baptiste, that you are indeed a liar and a complete fraud. Your story is nonsense and I ask you why you have concocted this rubbish?'

'That is extremely offensive, Mr Longworth. One day soon you may regret that comment.'

Longworth smirked as he made his next statement.

'I must tell you that we have attempted to contact heaven using the number you supplied and there was no response whatsoever. We also contacted British Telecom who have declared that it is impossible to contact heaven by any electronic means whatsoever. What do you say to that?'

'What is impossible for one person is not necessarily impossible for another. We are all different and we have different capabilities. YOU cannot understand the Super String Theory, but others have no difficulty. YOU are unable to become the Archbishop of Canterbury, but someone certainly will. Surely if God wanted to pass a message to the whole planet, he wouldn't contact every single person? Isn't it more likely that he would send a prophet with a message? This is one way, at least historically, how heaven communicated with the people of earth. As to the possibility of such communication, do you not believe in the miracles that Jesus Christ performed? If a man can cure a terminally sick person just by placing his hands on their head, or feed five thousand people with just five loaves of bread and two fish, then surely anything is possible, even ringing someone in heaven.'

'I deal with the real world, Mr Baptiste, not an imaginary world or a world of myths and legends. I just don't find anything you say in the least convincing. I ask you again why you made up this nonsense?'

'Have you not heard of Jacob's ladder, Mr Longworth?'

'No.'

'Then I suggest that your lack of biblical knowledge does not qualify you to pronounce on a matter such as this. You are an ignorant and prejudiced man.'

Longworth ignored this and instead of answering he changed direction.

'Let us return to the question of your alleged telephone conversation with the angel. What was the point of the conversation?'

'It was to tell me that I had been selected to pass on a message to the people of this country.'

'This gets better and better. What was the message?'

'It was to warn the people of this country that the world will be ending in about six months' time. My warning will provide an opportunity for people to repent before the Apocalypse.'

Longworth laughed and asked: 'and why is God going to destroy the world?'

'Because the people of the world have almost entirely disobeyed God's rules and recommendations for a just and spiritual life. You yourself report the atrocities of mankind daily and must be aware of the abysmal behaviour of mankind at all levels, from the highest in the lands to the lowest. Mankind is destroying the world and everything in it.'

Longworth smiled another of his derisory smiles. Then he laughed.

'This is hardly new. We have heard it before on numerous occasions and yet the world is still here. Do you really believe this nonsense?'

'I do.'

'And why should you be chosen above all other people to deliver this message? I would have expected a message from some entity in heaven to be delivered to a senior cleric rather than an insignificant person such as yourself.'

'So, would I. It came as a great shock to me but also a great honour. Reflect also that historically God communicates with the humble people of earth, not the high and the mighty. But tell me, Mr Longworth, on what authority do *you* choose to anticipate the working of heaven?'

'I base my opinions on common sense.'

'Common sense? I think not, but certainly common prejudice.'

Again, Longworth ignored my comment. 'Tell me what form this Apocalypse will take.'

'I don't know. I asked Sariel but either he didn't know or wouldn't tell me.'

'Were you told to pass on recommendations to the population as to what they should do before the end comes?'

'No, but like so much in life what the individual does is his own responsibility, so surely a prudent man would make peace with his creator?'

'So, to summarize, Mr Baptiste, you claim to have received a message from an angel in heaven directing you to tell the world that its destruction is imminent?'

'Not the whole world, just the people of this country. I was informed that there would be others chosen to pass on the same message in all the other countries. By the way I think that an apology is due from you for your offensive remarks.'

Longworth gave me a scornful look.

'I will be only too pleased to apologise when the earth is destroyed. Thank you, Mr Baptiste.'

He turned to the camera and smirked. 'There we have it – a prediction from heaven by an old man who dreams – that the world will end within six months. All I can say, ladies and gentlemen,' here he paused and smirked again, 'all I can say is that we make our peace with God.'

'And so say I,' I put in quickly.

I left the interview feeling quite pleased. Much to my surprise my feelings of terror at being interviewed had dissipated during the interview and I felt that I had done a reasonable job. It had gone better than I expected, and I wondered what the response to the broadcasting of my interview would be. I felt tired and the heat of the day made it worse; I was keen to go home and rest.

At home I had hardly sat down before the telephone rang. It was a caller claiming to be the Archangel Sariel who wanted to discuss the end of the world with me. It was a hoax, of course, but over the next few hours I received many such calls and eventually I just disconnected the phone.

I fell asleep and woke up two hours later in time to hear the main news. The usual political bickering was the first item followed by the usual violence on the streets. The unusually hot weather was also mentioned with the weather forecaster claiming that it was expected to last for some time. The penultimate item was interesting to me. I'm fascinated by astronomy and paid attention when I heard the newsreader say that astronomers reported that the previous night the stars had not twinkled. They believed that the light from the sun was being obstructed or deflected by some form of cloud. It was claimed that since the stars everywhere had not twinkled, this cloud must affect the whole earth. What was even more surprising was that nothing had been detected. The cloud defied analysis since distant spectroscopic examination proved to be negative. It was suggested that this cloud was responsible for the unseemly hot weather by acting as a sort of super-efficient greenhouse gas. It was expected, or so scientific experts agreed, that the weather would cool down as soon as the cloud dispersed. The final item on the news was my interview and it was presented as a form of entertainment to lighten the more serious news items. The smile on the face of the newsreader was exactly as I had expected and, apart from some slight disappointment, it had little effect on me.

The following day I felt obliged to return some of the calls I had previously received and ignored. Most were abusive, some were worried, and a few accused me of being a comedian. Two had wanted me to attend interviews and this I readily agreed to despite knowing that they would almost certainly be like my interview at the BBC. Almost all the people with whom I spoke refused to believe my prediction however, and their responses were derogatory and cynical; a few were openly offensive. Many of the telephone callers refused to believe that I had held discussions with an angel and when I persisted with my story, they, like many others, turned to verbal abuse. I found that just turning the telephone off was the best way of dealing with them. I had some sympathies with them. After all, I had been disbelieving, and it would be unreasonable for me to expect others to readily believe what I had found so difficult to accept. A few, just a few, were sympathetic and friendly and of these all with one exception were nutters – the sort of people who believed they had seen flying saucers or held discussions with alien life forms. The exception was an elderly vicar who was fascinated by my story and sympathetic to my predicament. Although he did not say that he believed me, he did at least admit to the possibility of it happening. Surprisingly perhaps, I heard nothing from any senior cleric. To them

I must have seemed like a head case in need of a care worker, someone to be pitied and ignored. Somehow, I dealt with all the calls without much difficulty. Archangel Sariel had been right and with no experience of speaking in public the appropriate words had come to me. Again, I felt that I had acquitted myself reasonably well.

The almost universally negative reaction was to be expected, of course, but the publicity gained from all the interviews and telephone calls helped me achieve my objective of publicising God's forecast. I quickly became famous, or rather notorious, throughout Great Britain, and I knew that my task had been fulfilled. Notoriety was of no consequence to me; all I wanted was to make people aware of the approaching Apocalypse. I was not alone in this and had reason to believe that the other prophets in all the other countries invariably found the same reaction. In fact, the worldwide nature of the prediction did eventually convince people of its authenticity.

With each passing day the temperature rose and after a week the scientists concluded that the effect of the cloud was not diminishing but increasing. The stars had completely disappeared after one week and the remarkable greenhouse properties of the cloud were quickly confirmed. It was clear to the scientists before anyone else that the cloud represented a threat to humanity, although they continued to hope that the world would completely pass through the cloud at any time, leading to a rapid return to normality.

The heat quickly became not just oppressive but debilitating for everyone. People everywhere suffered from sunstroke, heat exhaustion and burned skin. The farmers complained about the dryness of their fields and the desperate necessity for rain. The demand for water rose and rose as conditions deteriorated and the reservoirs were rapidly being depleted. In the House of Commons questions were asked about the weather and the Minister for Rural Affairs attempted to allay fears by reporting that all was well and that the country had sufficient reserves of water for at least three months.

Other countries were also suffering and those countries close to the equator were already in a perilous condition. The countries nearer the poles were, of course, considerably cooler and some wealthy people living in hot climates began a migration to the cooler areas of the planet, some even venturing as far as the polar regions.

In the week that followed there was no sign of the cloud dispersing and the temperature everywhere rose to unprecedented levels. Daytime temperatures of fifty degrees centigrade were common in Britain and people began to suffer. Normal work inside buildings was impossible unless an efficient air-conditioning system was operating, but as the temperatures rose still further, many of these systems broke down. It soon became impossible to work outside and gradually all daytime work ceased. The farmers were compelled to work at night. The post was not delivered until night-time, policemen were not seen in the streets and not surprisingly there was almost no crime during the day. Most people stayed at home out of the sunlight – to do anything else was impossible. The shops began to close during the hours of daylight and when supermarkets, grocers, butchers, bakers and all those who supplied food were unable to work during the day they opened for a restricted time at night. The hoarding of food became commonplace and soon all the shops had been emptied of the little they had. Deliveries of goods only occurred during the night-time and then ceased altogether. Stocks of food ran out and crime rose again.

Fires became commonplace and spread with alarming speed; what little water there was could not be spared to put them out. The dust and smoke from the burning fields and moors caused endless respiratory problems and doctors and hospitals were inundated with demands for help. Heat exhaustion was commonplace. People began to die. In response the Government pledged money to charter ships to sail to the polar regions and bring back huge quantities of arctic ice, but events proved to be deteriorating too quickly for the scheme to be implemented and it was quickly abandoned.

My telephone continued to ring and ring as more and more people changed their attitude to Sariel's prediction of catastrophe. This was no cause for any satisfaction on my behalf, but I did ring the BBC and ask whether I could be given a second interview with Mr Longworth. It was refused on the pretext that he was not available.

After three months of rising temperatures the death rate everywhere continued to rise, and I was once more phoned by increasing numbers of clerics. Apparently, at long last they were starting to believe that there was a real possibility of the world ceasing to have any life and they were greatly interested in my prediction. Belief in the Apocalypse was being accepted and all agreed to preach that salvation lay in paying homage to God and praying for their sins to be forgiven. The churches were full again to overflowing at the night-time services with people asking for forgiveness for their sinful lives. They recognised that soon they would be required to justify themselves before their maker. In these services the clergy prayed, begged and pleaded in vain for God to act and remove the cloud. Christenings and baptisms rose to unbelievable heights as the people of Great Britain came at last to believe that my warning was indeed accurate.

After four months the temperatures had risen to sixty degrees centigrade. The earth was parched, and great cracks began opening in the ground. The crops had failed totally and lay yellow and bone-dry in the fields. The cattle lay dead in their fields, their carcases gradually becoming nothing but bones covered with dry leather. No one cared and they remained unburied. Diseases became endemic and doctors were unable to help. The reservoirs were pronounced almost empty and water was available for just ten minutes in each day. Enormous quantities of water evaporated from the oceans of the world and the humidity in the atmosphere rose to 100% causing the discomfort and pain to rise to unbearable levels.

Television programmes were severely restricted and consisted only of news items at noon and midnight. What little could be learnt about the plight of other countries showed only that they were faring equally badly. Soon all transmissions ceased without warning.

Travel was impossible: all private and public transport had long since ceased and the blistering tarmac in the roads gave rise to great bubbles of noxious gases as it melted. Concrete structures cracked in the appalling heat, making them too dangerous to inhabit. Volcanoes erupted with far greater force than usual and vast clouds of poisonous fumes and ashes were discharged into the atmosphere. Earthquakes became commonplace leading to huge tracts of land being destroyed and the wholesale destruction of many villages and towns. People died everywhere: the old, the young, the humblest in the land and those who enjoyed the greatest privileges. Wealth was of no benefit. The heat was far too intense for anyone to help the stricken. Even the clergy were too prostate with desiccation and pain themselves to be able to help others worse off. The bodies lay where they had died, and no one cared or was able to bury them.

I suffered at least as much as anyone else, but my distress was perhaps greater because in some unfathomable and illogical way I felt responsible for the situation. I hadn't caused it, but I was intimately concerned with it. Could

I perhaps have pleaded with Archangel Sariel to apply to God for just one more chance? But even as I thought about it, I realised that he would have been unable to intercede on humanity's behalf even if he had been willing to do so. What could I do but pray to God for forgiveness for my own sins and forgiveness for mankind's collective sins? I hoped that all of mankind was praying for its own forgiveness.

After the fifth month all communication everywhere had ceased. There was no water, except in the atmosphere, and blistering drought lay over every land. No one ventured out in a fruitless search for water even at night. From my house I could see the land burning, the flames leaping up and falling away as the trees and bushes were consumed. In the far distance there was a huge fire covering many acres which could only have been Chester. I imagined that most of the countryside was now aflame and I could see and feel that the flames were coming ever closer to me. It had become commonplace to hear of explosions from industrial complexes where the stored chemicals autoignited and toxic fumes were discharged into the already poisonous atmosphere. Even in the countryside the air was full of the dust from burning materials, toxic chemicals and the stench of burning animals. By then the temperature had stabilised at sixty-three degrees centigrade, but this stabilisation had not led to any improvement in the situation.

My own condition was poor and getting worse. I had no water or food that was edible. My mouth was parched, and large red sores had appeared on my face as my body cried out for water to quench the dreadful heat. My mind was befuddled by the difficulty I had in tolerating the pain which racked my body and breathing in the hot, poisonous air. My lungs felt scorched every time I took a breath. I had great difficulty in moving, not that it mattered anyway as I had no reason to move, and I knew that the end could not be far away. It was night-time but the world outside my window was brightly lit by the flickering roaring flames as the fires remorselessly approached. I thought of Dante's Inferno again and wondered whether his vision of hell was like this flaming world. The flames spread rapidly and soon I could hear the house beginning to burn. I was too weak to care and almost too weak to move as I watched the flames come closer and closer to me. I started to choke on the burning debris in the scorching air and feeling an intense pain in my legs I saw the flames just start to lick at my feet. I cried aloud to God to help me and then to my amazement I saw a ladder materialise in front of me. It stretched through the ceilings and upwards towards heaven and I knew that Archangel Sariel had kept his word. With my last vestiges of strength, I gripped the lowest rung of the ladder and slowly, ever so slowly, began to climb.

10

IN THE END

Sometime after the earth had been destroyed by God as a punishment for mankind for not obeying his Commandments, the angels of the Third Choir were relaxing in the Garden of Eden. Their relief that the garden was unchanged and as beautiful as ever was evident. Once again, they could enjoy the simple and relaxing pleasures that the garden offered. The garden was exceptionally large and contained within it all the features that made for a perfect parkland. There were mountains, forests, woods, fields and lakes all embellished with choice flowers and shrubs. Unlike an earthly garden there were no seasons, and flowers, shrubs and trees all bloomed together. The scent of exquisite floral perfumes was everywhere in the pleasure gardens, and the forests and woods were filled with that delightful, earthy, nutty smell of trees and leaves that had been so prevalent on earth. The lakes were always popular and the walks beside them invariably led to places which resembled 'squares' in the cities that had once existed on earth. In these squares were elaborately carved fountains and statues of saints and cherubs. No images of God or his angels were permitted. Many of the popular walks and intersections had been given names such as the Holy Way, the Path of Righteousness, the Right Way, Ascension Hill, Christmas Corner and so on and all led to places where angels gathered for discussions of serious matters such as any bridge hands they had played well or badly. The most popular of these places was Trinity Triangle (which had originally been called Trinity Square until some angel pointed out the greater relevance of the Trinity). Trinity Triangle was a place surrounded by passion flowers and was always extremely popular. It was here that the angels of the Third Choir gathered.

The angels should have been as happy as only happy angels can be, but an observant watcher would have seen furrowed brows and frowns. Some were   clasping their heads as though they were in pain – something was giving them headaches.

It was the senior Archangel Michael who was holding forth on a recent development.

'I will not criticize God under any circumstances,' he said. 'God is always right and if events appear to be out of kilter or we don't understand them it is because we are unable to appreciate the full ramifications of God's will.'

'We know that Michael,' replied Raphael, 'and we fully agree.' He paused for a moment and then continued: 'but there is no doubt that some things have changed for the worse since the earth was destroyed.'

'A pertinent and scorching comment if ever I heard one,' replied Michael dryly, knowing full well that the earth had been incinerated.

Archangel Uriel also looked unhappy. 'Yes,' he said, 'Archangel Sariel was saying to me only the other day that he doesn't know where he is going to get some of his electronic components from now, and his work will undoubtedly suffer. Our mobiles, too, were repaired by him but what happens if he cannot get the components? I can envisage a time soon when heaven has a major communication problem because we can't speak to each other except when we are in a meeting. Previously the components of these items had always come from earth, but that source has now dried up. I sincerely hope that we don't have to resort to keeping a notebook and pencil and, if we do, I have no idea where to keep them.'

Gabriel agreed. 'We don't eat any food as a rule, but it was a great pleasure to occasionally have a slice of angel cake or a biscuit or some nectar. I recall too that some other delicacies also occasionally found their way into heaven for all to enjoy as well. Once, and I must say that I cannot remember the reason why, I obtained and enjoyed a bottle of Moét et Chandon and I loved the experience of having bubbles up my nose.'

Raphael agreed. 'Gluttony is a sin, you know, Gabriel; you mustn't enjoy it too much. You are quite right though and there are other things as well. Where are we going to get our holy water from now? That always came from earth. The saints, too, need some items. Saint Peter, for instance, requires tables for his group at the Pearly Gates to put their things on.'

'And our Monopoly boards and bridge cards,' said Uriel. 'I know that God can make these things, but he is always so busy that I haven't the nerve to ask him.'

'No, you're quite right not to do so,' replied Michael, 'you would get a thick ear if you did. I know an angel who once asked God if he would be so kind as to make a few items such as those, and he got two thick ears and his wings clipped for his trouble. I wouldn't recommend it.'

The angels thought about the problem and the more they talked about it the clearer it became that there were quite a few items previously obtained from earth that from now on would be completely unobtainable. It appeared that the problem of accessing some items was going to be bigger than previously thought.

The end of their period of relaxation came as the bell rang and the angels left the Garden of Eden to recommence their celestial duties.

Sometime later the angels of the Third Choir were surprised to receive a summons to a meeting with God. They assembled in the Design Conference Room as requested at the appointed time and soon afterwards God appeared.

'Angels of the Third Choir,' said God. 'We are here because of all my angels you are the most practical and I have a task for you which requires a practical bent.'

The angels breathed a sigh of relief. When summoned to these sorts of meetings they never knew the reason in advance. It might have been for a tribute for some work well done or it might have been for precisely the opposite reason. Clearly this was neither.

'As you are well aware, that pesky little planet, earth, has been destroyed,' continued God. 'The creatures called mankind which you, as a team, designed so long ago have proved to be complete duds. As a race the mortals of earth have been wilful, self-opinionated, far too concerned with themselves, ignorant, crude, addicted to violence, bloodthirsty, greedy, inclined to lie on every possible occasion, obsessed with reproduction and, undoubtedly the worse trait of all, not in the slightest interested in spiritual matters and the well-being of others. In their favour I can only say that they are industrious and ingenious. This record can only be described as a great disappointment and I have given it a mark of omega minus.

'The blame for this cannot be laid at your feet. Physically mankind has achieved everything the design intended. It is the spiritual side where failure has been so pronounced. At the time of construction men and women were fitted with the mark ten brain. Subsequent events have proved this brain to be defective, but when mankind was created it was the best available. It was withdrawn from use shortly afterwards and now we have far better brains, more concerned with spiritual matters and less prone to breakdown.

'Heaven generously provided considerable help, but throughout its history mankind thought it knew better and ignored our advice and developed a pronounced determination to move to the dark side of existence, namely non-existence. Far too many of their people have gone to hell. In view of all this I had no option but to destroy the earth and all that was in it.

'Earth has gone, but now I find that the symmetry of my universe has been disturbed. There is a hole in the galaxy known as the Milky Way where the earth was, and where no hole should be. The question that now arises and the one I put to you all is: what do we put in the hole? It needs to be filled with something and preferably something which looks pretty and shiny. Do I make another planet? If so, what sort do you recommend? Should I then design other creatures to occupy this new planet? Shall I fill it with energy and turn it into a galactic firework display? Shall I put a black hole there?

'I wish you to consider this matter and prepare a report (in triplicate, of course) for me as soon as possible.'

God then disappeared in a slight puff of wind and the angels were left looking at each other in amazement.

'Well,' said Archangel Michael. 'That was a surprise.'

'I'm so relieved that the defects of mankind are not our fault after all,' said Raphael. 'I was having difficulty in sleeping caused by worrying about that.'

'Me too, matey,' cried all the others and the relief they all felt was palpable.

'But how on earth do we approach this problem?' asked Uriel

'Don't say "on earth" any more please, Uriel,' said Michael. 'It is inappropriate from now on.'

The angels turned their attention to the problem they had been given but although they were the most practical of the angels, they were still divine and occasionally struggled with physical concepts. At first they considered the concept of making the space where the earth had been into a place of entertainment – a sort of celestial Imax holographic cinema – but as the universe was expanding at an enormous rate of knots they thought that it would be used fewer and fewer times until eventually it would be completely unused, and the idea was soon abandoned as a celestial white elephant. The same argument applied to any sort of light show whether it was thunder and lightning shows or marvels of the universe or firework displays or whatever.

They considered the expansion of heaven into the same space that earth had occupied. The end of the earth had meant that some billions of new souls were all attempting to enter heaven. They had done nothing but argue and fight each other and Saint Peter had suffered from a series of breakdowns from all the extra aggravation and the work involved in finding accommodation for them, and this housing problem had still to be resolved. The idea that the place where earth had once been (when occupied by living humans) should be converted into a haven for the souls of those same humans, might well be poetic justice but it would also be an example of extreme irony.

'The problem,' remarked Raphael, 'is that we don't have any biscuits to help us think and generate ideas. I could really do with a chocolate cream right now,'

The others all chorused agreement and a pointless wish for sugar-laden biscuits was made by all.

Without biscuits the angels felt hampered and yet ideas still appeared. Another suggestion was to create a black hole where the earth had been. This could then be used as a dump for all the waste that was generated from other planets but again this was abandoned due to the distances the waste would have to travel. The problem of constructing a black hole would also have the disadvantage of destabilising the solar system, or having to redesign it completely, and once more this idea was abandoned.

After some considerable thought they concluded that God should consider designing another planet, but common sense told them that any new planet would have to be almost identical to earth. If it departed from earth's specification too much, then the whole of the solar system would be in a state of imbalance and this could lead to other and far more serious problems. Not only that but another planet would probably need other forms of life and that meant that God would have to spend much time designing and creating more life forms, and they doubted whether that would be popular.

The angels made suggestion after suggestion but still

nothing appropriate was forthcoming, and eventually Archangel Michael suggested they end the meeting, and let their minds dwell on other matters. If their subconscious minds dwelt on the problem while they slept then someone might have a rush of brains to their head and come up with the goods.

In fact, the solution came to Archangel Michael later when he was having his wings cleaned in the wing-cleaning department.

He leapt off the small cloud he was sitting on and shouted: 'YES, YES.'

'Steady, steady,' said the pinion refurbishment angel crossly as he had just been jolted into nicking himself with his pinking scissors.

'But I have the solution,' cried Michael happily.

At the first available moment he sent a text message to all the Third Choir angels saying that he knew what to do with earth's space and could they assemble as quickly as possible. Having come to believe that they had been handed a poisoned chalice and that no satisfactory solution would ever be found, the others flew to the Design Conference Centre with considerable alacrity and sat on the small clouds that acted as seats. When all were present and paying attention, Michael addressed the meeting.

'Angels. I have a proposal to put to you about the task which God has set us. It will, I'm sure, resolve all our problems at a stroke.'

The others all smiled to one another, put their hands

together and prayed that he was right.

Michael then went on to describe his idea. The others considered it, turned it inside out until it looked like a Möbius strip, dissected it, reconfigured it, discussed it, and then thoroughly endorsed the whole idea.

'Brilliant,' said Raphael.

'Brilliant,' said Uriel.

'Brilliant,' said Gabriel.

'Pack it up you lot,' growled Michael. 'What we need to do now is to consolidate our ideas and then present them as a report to God.'

'In triplicate?' asked a minor angel.

'Of course,' replied Michael. 'You should know that all reports are done in triplicate except, of course, the ones marked PRIVATE – FOR GOD'S EYES ONLY.'

They readily agreed to Michael's suggestion before girding their loins and considering the details. How much detail was required for the land masses? What should the roofs of the sheds be made of? Who would operate the machinery?

It took a long time and with nothing but the limited supply of holy water to refresh themselves they all felt weary and spent when the final report (in triplicate) was in front of them.

'Well. Thank goodness, that's done at last,' said Michael.

He sent a text to God saying that their report was ready for his scrutiny and almost immediately received a reply to go to God's suite of rooms at once.

There God read the report three times and smiled.

'Excellent,' he said, and his eyes twinkled. 'There is a symmetry about this that is most appealing. I shall make the arrangements at once. There will be much material to obtain.'

The arrangements were indeed on a large scale. Huge quantities of earth, stone of all types, water and so on which would be required for the construction of the planet (which would be an exact replica of earth in terms of size and composition), were ordered and delivered and the group of angels known for their terraforming skills quickly erected the planet. After that, bricks, mortar, shed roofing and machinery had to be ordered, delivered and erected according to the plans. It was a big job, but one which God had carried out many times before and he knew exactly what he was doing. Some of the less cerebral angels were detailed as workers in the new buildings and required to undergo various courses of instruction. It all proceeded quickly and within a very respectable time everything was ready for the grand opening.

It was the custom in heaven that when a new planet or planetary system was created an opening ceremony marked the occasion. God was far too busy to perform the opening ceremony himself, but he had detailed one of the Seraphim to act on his behalf. The ceremony was rather low-key and brief, as befitted a minor planet, but none the less effective. Archangel Sariel's giant screens were once again erected and the few angels who were interested were permitted time off from their celestial duties to watch the ceremony.

On the new planet the Seraphim made the following speech: 'holy, holy, holy. By the authority invested in me by my Lord, God, I name this planet "Heart" and declare the factory open for business. May God bless it and all who work in it.'

There was a blast of heavenly trumpets, the Seraphim cut the ceremonial tape and the planet was revealed in all its glory, which wasn't much.

It consisted of a single mass of land which occupied half of the planet; the other half consisted of water. The land was devoid of any feature of interest: there were no mountains, valleys, forests, deserts or anything of agricultural interest. On this flat landscape, whose flatness was reminiscent of East Anglia on the old earth, was a huge factory. Despite its appearance as a single large factory, within it were several smaller ones, each dedicated to the manufacture of some item required in heaven. There were factories for the manufacture of playing cards, Monopoly boards, tables and one solely devoted to the provision of electronic items. Another small factory was devoted to the preparation of holy water. The largest factory of all was devoted to the provision of those items closest to the hearts of the angels: it made biscuits. It not only made biscuits, but every type of biscuit ever made. There were custard creams, Bourbons, digestive biscuits, Waggon Wheels, Jaffa cakes, Florentines, macaroons, flat biscuits, round biscuits, straight biscuits, curly biscuits and every type of wafer possible.

When the angels saw the list of products which would be made, a great cheer rang out in heaven. The angels sang the praises of God and all was happiness and light.

What had once been the planet earth was now a planet devoted solely to the manufacture of goods, and particularly biscuits, essential to the angelic host in heaven.